THE

OF

LOST

INTENTIONS

A
GUIDE FOR THE
ARTISTICALLY WAYLAID

A. VALLIARD

Copyright Pedantry

'Standing Bacchus' on the rear cover is by an anonymous artist, from the Royal Museum of Fine Arts, Antwerp, photo by Studio Philippe de Formanoir – Paso Doble, and the King Baudouin Foundation, and licensed under CC BY-SA 4.0.
'The Sunmiler' was first published in Cordite Poetry Review.
Cover by A. Valliard, using creative commons imagery, purchased elements, and items from the splendid Rawpixel.
Ink Stamps, Blots, & Splatters by A. Valliard & MiksKS.
Typeset utilising typefaces EB Garamond, IM FELL English, BogArt Deco, More Aloof, Roxelane, and a panoply of ludicrous drop caps too numerous to mention.

ISBN 978-0-9756457-0-3 (Paperback)
www.thecityoflostintentions.com
©VAROQUE BOOKS 2024

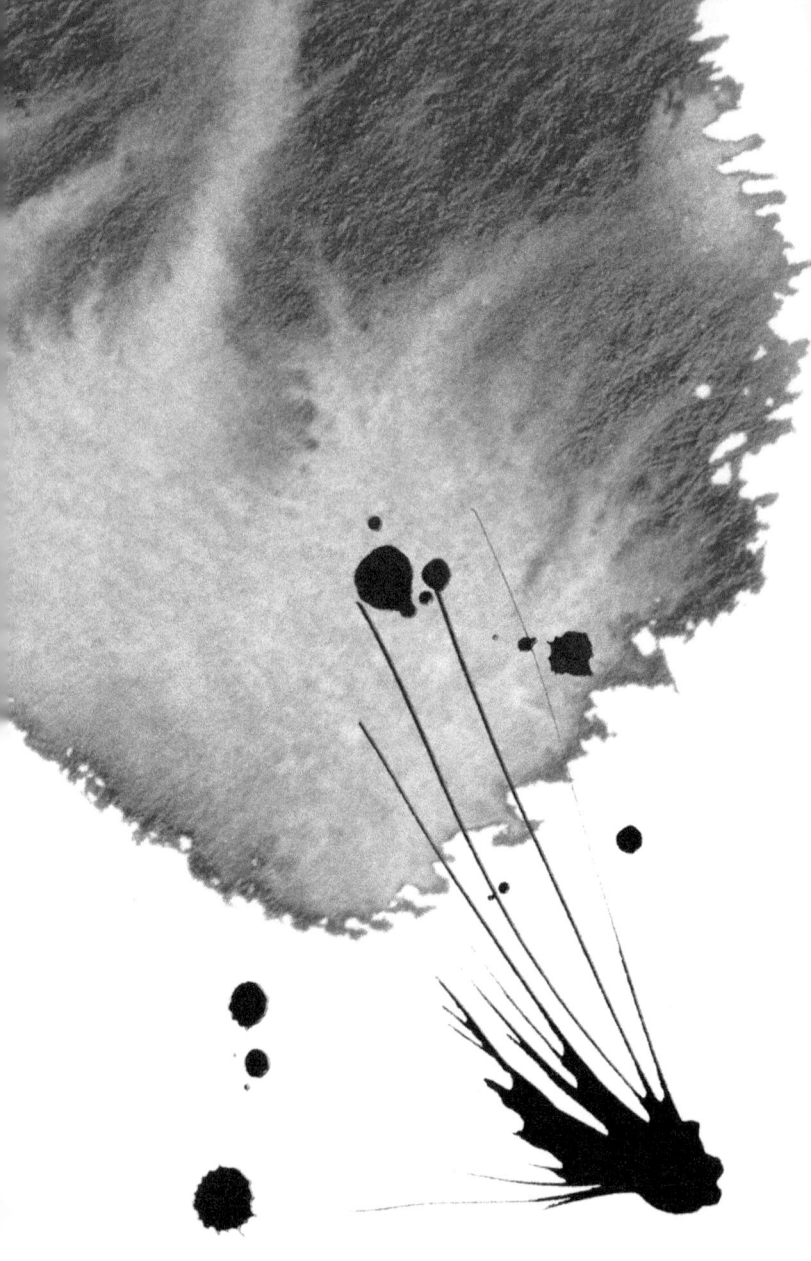

For my Fellow Self-Saboteurs.

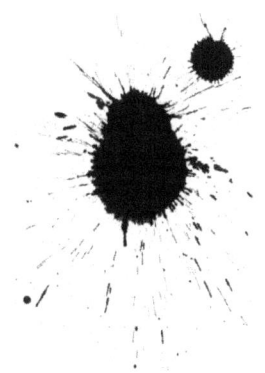

PREAMBLE

OMEWHERE, SLIPPED BETWEEN THE PAGES OF REALITY, LIES A LAND OF ETERNAL CARNATION.

Within its unbound borders, the Inkspill Sea stretches infinitely in one direction, and the dunes of the Just Desert stretch infinitely in the other. At least, we think they're infinite. We're not going to go out and check.

In the middle, where ink and sand meld, is a questionable metropolis, seething under a dome of glass. From outside, this city is invisible.

Until you come to it—or worse, it comes to you—

and by then, alas, it is far too late.

Too late for what? You might ask, a trifle irritated.

Too late for you.

Have you sullied your artistic Vision? Frittered away your talents? Been swallowed by envy, or led by fear or fame astray? Ignored the terrifying and frankly unreasonable demands of your soul?

Then welcome to the City of Lost Intentions, home of those who have betrayed their Hearts! A realm of withered pursuits and abandoned quarries. The squandered wealth, *incalculable*.

One is sent here by internal tribunal.

You had one mortal life, a single gold coin with which to buy your eternal form. Or, if you prefer, as you wrote your worldly part, such will be your endless play. Whether farce or tragedy, the story is yours, acted by you alone, interminably.

It's all rather unpleasant.

But your Heart doesn't care. After all, it dispatched you here.

Life is meaningful because the Heart makes it so.

At death, the soul continues on, in art, in act, in memory; a rippling of the spirit over the waters of eternity. But those artists who have betrayed their Heart's great Vision continue here instead, as though in a book slammed shut upon their character, leaving them trapped in their pivotal, defining scene.

They become Carnations: the Eternally Carnated. Transmogrified into creatures bearing the foul or fair nature of their insult to their art. Their souls twisted into the form they chose—forever.

This guidebook presents the idly curious, the armchair traveller—or indeed, prospective resident—with a rogues' gallery of these rapscallions, as viewed from the perspective of a penitential tourist. For sometimes the Heart sends its owner here as a warning shot across the bow, that they may learn how to dodge a horrible, if faintly ludicrous, fate.

Appropriately, a granted not-so-horrible but equally ludicrous Guide accompanies them on their journey through the metropolis and its arenas of artistic crime.

There is Avoidance, Neglect, Infidelity, Diminishment, Contortion, Desecration, Betrayal, Sabotage, Poisoning, and Abandonment. Populated by the Prevaricators, Pifflers, Panbacchanals, Pasquinades, Periwinklers, Pillagers, Punchinellos, Pyrrhics, Picksores, and Perilosts, respectively.

What is this plethora of Ps?

Alliteration.

Blame the Architect of this peculiar and lamentable affair. They have much to answer for already.

MONTCORBIER

THE GUIDE TO THIS CITY IS TALL—WHEN VERTICAL—POINTY AND DOLEFUL. A melancholy sundial who only counts the unhappy hours. He wears a frock coat the colour of despair, over which a tarnished gold embroidery creeps like a disease. There is a charm about him, tinged with a hint of potential disaster, like watching a tame lion gambol around a group of visiting schoolchildren.

He has an architectural face; an ornamental façade housing a soul of narrow corridors and vast empty ballrooms, through which a lonely, cold wind blows.

Montcorbier—for such is his name—is beautiful, but in the way poison bottles and oil slicks are beautiful. Or Gliophorus psittacinus, the parrot waxcap toadstool. His black locks are ill-kempt, and a faded yellow carnation wilts from his lapel. He is smeared with soot, which mingles unpleasantly with the powder on his hollow cheeks.

This haunted doll of a man is human, barely, but it has been so long since he has spoken with anyone except fallen artists, that he has rather lost his manners.

Unfortunately for all, he has found a sword to compensate, and a goatskin of stale Bordeaux lurches next to this regrettable épée.

He often lies (in more ways than one) upon a rock near the Inkspill Sea like a strand of wine-soaked seaweed in Turkish slippers. And he is your only hope of reaching the end of this city, for better or worse.

Almost certainly worse.

Whenever cadenced caterwauling comes from the shore, slowly and resentfully, his eyes will open. They are baleful, grey eyes, long-lashed and wandering. Glazed and eerie. Raw-rimmed. Not well. The eyes of a sleepwalker. They will roll. Close again. Distaste will contort his pallid features, as though someone has pinched the surface of a skin of milk.

An artist has washed up.

Possibly a poet.

Possibly yourself.

Poets would be the death of him (Montcorbier often says), were he not already dead. And probably in some arcane metre. Gods help him.

In the mean, he waits, and gods help you!

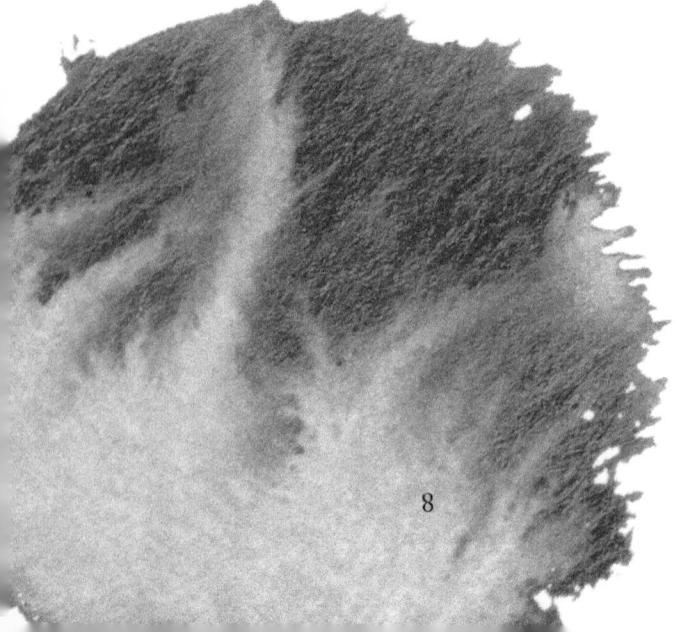

8

THE CROSSING

WHEN ONE HAS BEEN SO CARELESS AS TO BE DAMNED TO VISIT THE ETERNAL CARNATION, A GONG STRIKES ON HIGH TO ANNOUNCE YOUR ARRIVAL—HEARKEN!

At the sound of this invisible bronze monstrosity, the sea twitches as though stung. The reverberation dances over the black water and shudders in the deep.

The heavens turn sickly; a gelatinous oyster, then a bubbling olive. They bulge and tremble. Clouds form, corkscrew into a twister of candlesmoke and outspit the penitential tourist, or your goodly self.

9

Doomed Icarus! Flailing and shrieking, you plummet into the sea with a crack.

The waters yawn, and suck your wretched soul beneath. You churn below in the turbulent darkness, bob to the surface as flotsam, then out of the howling waves are flung. Hurled headlong from the Inkspill Sea!

As the shoreline is jagged with potsherds and broken statues, this is an unhappy entrance for you.

Haul yourself from the painful shallows, as if a poor creature from the ocean floor. Monster from a mariner's map. Beached!

Ink in your eyes. Your gullet. Your breadbasket. Your lights! Cough, and expel ink with a squirt like a fountain pen. Don't try to dry your ink-wet face with your ink-wet clothes. Abandon the charade.

Behold, instead, the alien landscape.

A smoking black beach is pressed into the dunes, flaked and layered like the charred pages of a manuscript. Upon this slate, waves of ink are drawing and withdrawing, leaving a wrack line of pigment scribbling along the coast.

In the air, ash floats on a stench of snuffed candlewick and tallow, mingling with the metallic miasma drifting from the sea. Labyrinthine roots writhe inland to disappear behind a fog bank, a Brobdingna-gian mainsail straining at its rigging.

This wall of vapour has its own peculiar odour; a

decaying floral sweetness which clings to the skin like the wrinkled petals of a rotten flower.

Nevertheless! Sway to your feet and stagger forward on seasick ankles. The fog will embrace you. We can't stop it. Clamber on over the roots, deeper into the haze, towards whatever horror lies beyond.

Force yourself forward through the clammy cloud, and you will encounter the glass walls of the realm itself. They will prove no barrier. Push, and they will admit you as easily as falling down a flight of black-painted stairs in the dark.

Once through, Montcorbier will be there to welcome you.

Condolences for this lamentable event.

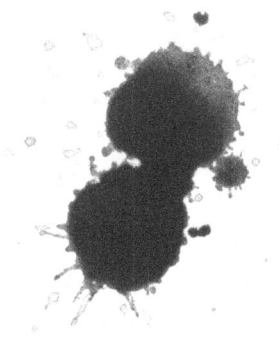

THE CITY OF LOST INTENTIONS

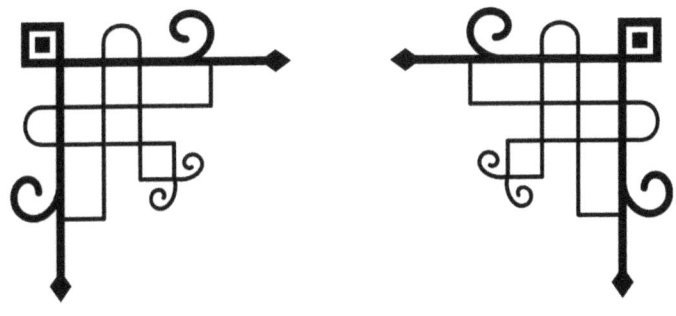

THE CITY OF LOST INTENTIONS

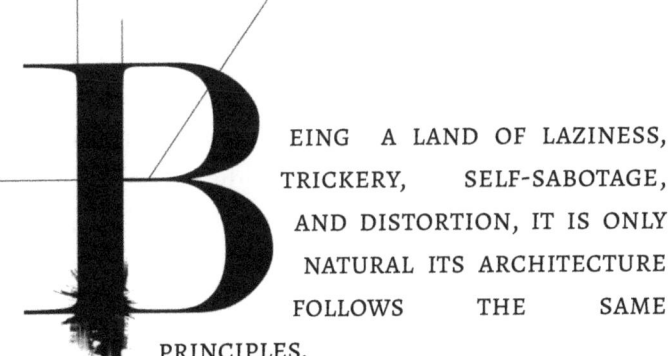

EING A LAND OF LAZINESS, TRICKERY, SELF-SABOTAGE, AND DISTORTION, IT IS ONLY NATURAL ITS ARCHITECTURE FOLLOWS THE SAME PRINCIPLES.

Behind the fortified walls of its sole city, obscure buildings swagger and lurk, rising tall above the ramparts, their spires and finials prickling the sky.

Some appear Baroque, some Mudéjar or Gothic, and others resemble the fever-dream of a bilious draughtsman.

Overwrought towers groan upwards on tilted foundations, and buttresses fly so high and in such unexpected and alarming directions they become hazardous to birdlife.

Grotesques dangle upside down facing the walls, and so grimace at no-one, and incomplete arches hover over alleyways, lacking keystones. Gates tempt with solid stone behind them, and staircases march triumphantly into nothingness.

Twisting and writhing around an elongated mountain, the city resembles nothing so much as a crazed croquembouche, lashed together with inordinate filigree. Cobbled streets rivulet down the slopes, glistening with an unhealthy film, cryptic flags slump upon their staffs (for the air is as still as stone) and in the heights, onion domes erupt like iridescent mushrooms, their cupolas swollen into unwieldy dimensions.

Above all, the sun hangs at its zenith, looming malign and motionless in the sky, baking the city in perpetuity.

And it is a terrible city, in an increasing state of peril. For its Architect had failed to be vigilant to their design, leaving it an unfinished, mangled thing. Forlorn, half mad, and dangerous.

Thus, as with all objects that demand constant attention, be it the Heart or an irrigation system, under neglect, pestilence has bred in the corners.

Rust crimps and bubbles the ironwork, and mould gluts itself on rotting wood. Verdigris creeps across copper rooftops, smothering them in fake vitality. Lichen thrives in the cornices. A lacy white fungus drapes over the awnings in a nightmarish web.

Enormous strangler vines roam the streets in vegetative idleness, wrapping themselves around pagodas, toppling pinnacles. The buildings pierce upwards through this slimy tangle of dank and dying foliage, which draws back like blackened gums, exposing the bones of the city.

Dented compasses, cogs and gears, and the twisted innards of clocks litter the boundaries, poking their metallic fangs up through the encroaching dunes of the Just Desert.

A moat of ink enwraps the whole. A noisome brew, far from the purity of the Inkspill Sea. Dark tentacles emerge from its murky depths, crawl up caked pigment banks, and leave lethargic stains upon the shoreline. Boats made of empty colour pots, palette skiffs, and water shakers, scud around the rim, dragged widdershins as though caught in a whirlpool.

In each sits a Peregrinator, the first Carnation you will see (albeit, fleetingly) upon this journey, its shiny brass astrolabe face forever amazed by what it sees.

But it can never disembark.

It can only witness the activity of this chaotic

columbarium of souls, and marvel at its intricacy from afar. For even the most jaded visitor must admit the city has a curious beauty, crowned by its golden domes nestling like spider eggs among whorled black spires, cloaked in a sulphurous sand blown in from the desert beyond.

The charred blast of dust mingles with the sweet tropical reek of rot and fermented fruit rising from the rank alleys, and it is this alone that mars the city's splendour, this stench of tragedy and decay drifting from its core, which curls up the hill carried on a rare coil of weary wind.

THE VAGUELS

ver the moat that surrounds the city, birdlike creatures swoop and soar. The idle and lost imaginings of the world, the Vaguels sew invisible patterns in the air as they group and break apart again. Abandoned ideas, penned, then flung away. Fleeting thoughts that fled for good. Musings that murmured into nothingness and dreams scratched with haste in the dim dawn, or utter darkness, only to reveal themselves indecipherable by day. The forgotten illuminations of the drunken hour.

These whims wing their way to the City of Lost Intentions, where they become a paper bird according to the nature of the contemplator. Thus, there are peeled-wine-label birds, origami-napkin birds, overdue-bill birds, marbled-endpaper birds, unheeded-court-summons birds, expensive-monogrammed-paper birds, flattened-cigarette-box birds, papyrus birds, and even carbon-copy birds which shadow each other's flight.

Starched or flimsy, coarse or gossamer, the Vaguels commingle in their murmuration, or drift in debonair elegance on the ink, preening themselves. Some warble amongst the swaying reed-brushes, or peck with moody malevolence at the joints of the bridge.

PILFERERS

own by the moatside, fishing rods waver in a row over the swirling black water, clicking and clashing together like the antennae of an irritable insect. The wielders of these poles are the Pilferers. Rodentesque varmints in patchwork rags which have trickled down from the Colonauseam to catch fresh ideas to flog at the stalls in the hypogeum.

Sudden excitement—

A haul!

Heaved onto the bank, a wet and glistening Purpose, its scales brighter than stars.

The Purpose flops around on the ebony sludge, bares its translucent, pointed teeth, unhinges its jaw, and swallows its captor.

A cheer goes up from the others.

THE SEAL OF APPROVAL

loating a leap away from the bank, an oversized ink dish bobs in the moat. Inside, a wonky individual composed of sealing wax clings to its oar, a long calligraphy brush it uses to pole new arrivals across the black waves.

Its winsome, red, intaglio-stamped face emits a shrill, cajoling, and somewhat waxy song.

The Seal is part of the city's mercifully small parcel of Uncivil Servants, of whom Montcorbier is also one, and it bears a yellow carnation upon its glossy personage to signify the fact (as does Montcorbier, however resentfully).

Montcorbier elects to cross by bridge, and he tells the Seal this daily, but the newly arrived tourist (or prospective resident) usually places one confident foot on the brim of the boat, windmills in panic and sits down immediately.

Black froth slaps at the prow—although the prow is difficult to tell in a circular vessel—as you set off, the Seal brush-poling at speed. The ink clears as you advance.

THE INKLINGS

f one peers over the side into the waves, amid the thrashing shadows will peer back, in various states of apathy, or delirium, or obliviousness, a collection of phosphorescent creatures. These are the unborn ideas and embryonic works of the world.

Some resemble seahorses or anemones; beautiful, fanciful, frail, and tendrilled. Others are more membranous and spiny, like pufferfish or urchins. Hideous, but interesting.

Very few will ever see the light of day.

Unseen, crawling along the bottom of the moat, creep the ever-scheming, warty Subconches.

THE VAINGUARDIANS

efore the city's encircling walls, a display of military ineptitude takes place. Throngs of Vainguardians, clad in an eclectic array of fabulous armour, enthusiastically attack the city, whilst another motley-armoured horde enthusiastically defend it.

A few enlightened individuals attack themselves for the sheer convenience. They fight themselves bravely as they roll down the banks, grappling with their own merciless grip.

On the parapets, more Vainguardians scuttle in utmost confusion, some raising standards only to lower them again. Others pour boiling oil from a machicolation in an ill-directed stream. Pennants are strung jauntily along the crenellations, then removed. Restrung. Ad infinitum.

Canons, set outside on the opposing moat bank, face the city. Every so often, a Vainguardian pulls the cord, jerking the canon upwards as it fires, then gazes aloft in earnest, seeking the lost projectile.

Against the battlement (whose alcoved arrow slits are naturally cut into the wrong side), rope ladders swing and tangle, each containing a screaming warrior.

In an inner courtyard, a Vainguardian is hefted into a trebuchet and then hurled over the walls, away from the city. Pilferers, interrupted in their fishing, drag the hapless projectile back over the bridge, and return it to the same baffled Vainguardians, who, several minutes later, once more fling their complaining comrade towards the banks.

Each Vainguardian also bears a yellow carnation displayed proudly upon its armour, signifying the wearer is part of the realm's apparatus.

And indeed they are.

The Vainguardians are the manifestly unhelpful Defenders of the Heart. For, it is said, metaphorically, that in the absence of external foes, the Heart sets in upon itself.

And as the City of Lost Intentions *is* the artist's Heart, in a manner of speaking, the Vainguardians have chosen to be stubbornly literal about their job.

THE SENTINEL (ON FIRE)

igh on the barbican stands the Sentinel (on Fire). Do note, this is a state of existence unadvantageous for a sentinel, or indeed for anyone.

A dying ember throbs in the Sentinel's chest and its head is a plume of blue light. It too wears a carnation, which is also on fire.

Beneath a crown of flames, the Sentinel's face remains impassive as it studies anyone entering the city. Its gaze and manner suggest it thinks them unworthy of studying.

If it agrees to let you in, which it believes it has the power to decide (it does not), the Sentinel crackles and hums. Miles away, a copse of dignified trees bursts into flame. Along the walls of the city, a tongue of fire gives a suspicious lick and then retreats, mollified. The blue of the Sentinel's head changes in a reluctant pulse to emerald.

It is meant to alert the city to threats (another useless venture) but in truth it has set the place ablaze times numberless.

THE CITY OF LOST INTENTIONS

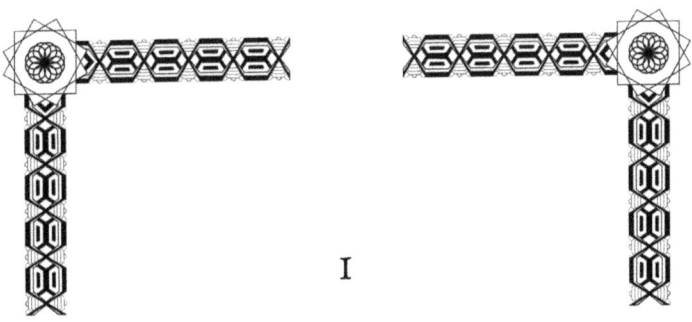

I

THE PIAZZA

AVOIDANCE OF ART

PREVARICATORS

AWNING BEYOND THE GATES OF THE CITY, A VAST ROUND PIAZZA BAKES IN THE ETERNAL NOONDAY SUN.

Pennants of dusky yellow brighten its ring of dark arcades, and paint peels and cracks on the warped window shutters above the bulbous, overhanging brows of balconies frowning at alarming angles.

At the centre of this space erupts a colossal hourglass, filled with blood-red sand. Procrastinators contort in its lower globe, limbs thrashing, drowning in an abundance of time.

And here we meet our first collection of Carnations: The Prevaricators.

Those who through fear of societal critique, or fear of a disappointing self-illumination, or fear of suffering in the pursuit of something wholly unreliable and entirely imaginary, had filled their lives with anything to avoid their art, and are now trapped in the form their avoidance took, forever.

There is a fourth type of fear, the most devastating, but it belongs in the Undermine, which we will get to, eventually.

In the meantime, every manner of miscreant cavorts within these walls, so let our visitor follow close behind Montcorbier as he weaves his seamless way through the lively tapestry, a tall and tattered barquentine sailing recklessly into a storm.

THE FLÂNEURS

Flouncing obscenely before the gate, leap the Flâneurs, buffeting the arrival with waves of nonsensical noise as they run the gauntlet of gossip.

Once artists who dandied their days away on the boulevard, the Flâneurs are now Carnated as delicate creatures made of lace and walking sticks, lashed together with silk stockings. Powder rises in cumulus clouds from their handkerchiefs as they cackle, witter and frou-frou away their talents.

They are beginning to shed, so watch where you step.

THE ATTACHÉ & TYCOON

Hurtling through the piazza on thin leather legs, the Attaché had been so caught up in important worldly business affairs it had no time for creative work. IT SAID NO TIME.

The Attaché comes in two styles: the Provincial Mayor, made of a soft, high quality, overworked Italian cowhide, with very mournful eyelets, and prone to wistfully, publicly yearning for a garret and an artistic lifestyle.

And its latter-day counterpart, the Tycoon, passing by with the speed of a thousand gods.

The Tycoon has a split, rectangular head of shiny black snakeskin, and bronze clasps for ears. Its paper face riffles like a flip book through expressions of dread, rage, doubt, and frustration. Its jacket opens and sheaves of documents fall out. It spins and stops to gather them with haste, and runs on. They tumble out again. A cloud of paper blooms in its wake.

THE LAURELRESTER

 arved from a single large shiny bay leaf, the aromatic Laurelrester circumnavigates the piazza on a perpetual book tour, hoisted aloft on a sedan chair made of presentation copies. It flogs its bearers—four harried lecterns—with passion.

In soul-curdling terror of the infamous 'difficult second work', the Laurelrester had decided not to *write* the second, but instead to talk loud and long about the first, hoping to die before its reputation did.

THE SOAPBOXERS

eetering on homemade plinths, a variety of transparent Soapboxers noiselessly harangue their imaginary awed audience.

Enchanting, iridescent bubbles pour from their open, silent mouths, as they gulp like goldfish.

The Soapboxer had opinions and was very good at ventilating them. It did this in grateful preference to being cloistered alone with its Vision.

THE AFFRONTED

A midst the bubbles leaps the Affronted, slashing at each and all. Built like an oversize burr, in life it found many things to rub it the wrong way. When peace means confronting one's art, the world is full of battles.

The Affronted lassoes its thorny arms around in rage.

THE CLAMOUR

irst there is a hideous, grinding noise on the peripheries, then abruptly, with a metallic screech, a flickering, fluctuating figure appears, bringing all Sturm und Drang with it, and several cymbals.

In a shining, painted face, its bright eye contains a despairing glint of hope. Its pinwheel hat spins with a whirr.

The Clamour once did anything to drown out the voice in its head, which told it that time was passing, and in the face of a godless universe it must devote itself to art. It did, in fact, anything *except* devote itself to art.

It opens its round mouth in an agonised wail. Higher and higher rises the scream until it ends in the blare of a klaxon.

THE MILLINEED

oiled unhappily on the cobblestones, the Millineed heaves a hollow sigh.

One of the creature's legs wants sea, another dry land. One wants adventure, another stillness and reflection. Once it has chosen, it can begin its work. But which to choose?

Poor wretch of conflicting wants, tormented by desire for all! If it had set its Heart on any of them, it wouldn't have a foot in this joint, but alas, now it is stuck here, prevaricating forever, frozen with indecision.

The Millineed weeps out of its many tiny eyes.

THE KNACKERY

earby, a centaur drags a barrow of stones around in a circle, to no end. Its face holds a look of quiet and mournful resolve. Sweat beads on its ropey haunches.

The Knackery took refuge from the demands of its art in needless physical labour. It ensured it was far too exhausted to confront its Vision. It wore itself to the bone sooner than pick up a quill.

THE AMANUISANCE

hattering whilst scribbling into a minuscule notebook, the Amanuisance is Carnated as a simian scribe attached to the back of an oblivious stone Colossus.

The parasitical passenger points out various directions it hopes the narrative might go, ignored by the Colossus, which continues to blunder on as it wishes.

A pleasing symbiosis might have occurred had this artist who chose to avoid its art through slavish transcription of the lives of other artists attached itself to a Carnation which avoided its art by talking about it. Unfortunately, the Amanuisance didn't want to be upstaged, so it had chosen a strong but unhelpfully silent type.

The Colossus itself had been a Palaeolithic artist, and was not especially prone to chronic and neurotic self-flagellation, so its presence in a hell where admission relies on guilt and self-damnation, is a matter most perplexing.

THE UPROAR

arching clockwise, a mammoth porcupine bristling with blank signs, fictitious flags, and illegible manifestos is on never-ending parade.

There is an unfathomable amount of injustice in the world, and surely, fighting injustice is more immediately useful and honourable than devotion to one's art?

Indeed, possibly! Almost certainly!

But the Uproar didn't march for that. It fled in fear from its Vision.

THE ROUSE

ehind the Uproar honks the Rouse, its ears flattened back against a narrow skull that widens out to a gigantic megaphone at the front.

The Rouse lived to alert society to danger—an act infinitely more exciting and less frightening than pursuing its art. It thrilled to see chaos in its wake and thrived under the attention reaped by being the messenger. That one day someone would probably shoot the messenger only added to its enjoyment.

THE KNIGHT ERRAND

igh and bright, a trumpet ta-tarrahs, and a splendid suit of armour hoves into view.

Mounted on a horse draped in rich, illuminated parchment, the Knight Errand advances in a haughty trot across the pavings. The sharp clop of iron on stone, and restless slop of chain mail, resounds even above the general piazza hubbub.

The suit of armour holds a jousting quill. Its banderole, a shred of blotting paper. It is a majestic idiot, its helmet plumed and impractical.

Behold the Knight Errand on its relentless quest to flee its work! In life, when no target for its quest existed, it created one! The quest was noble. Or the quest was going down the shops, or devoted to collecting antique swords or porcelain elephants, but the Knight called it noble!

THE HABERDASH

Whenever the Knight Errand is feeling fractious, which is often, it will fight the Haberdash, a silk-suited dressmaker's dummy astride an iridescent stag beetle with rhinestoned antennae.

The Haberdash avoided inward attention to its art through outward attention to itself. Its blank head balances like an egg on a ruff of risible dimensions. Spangles infect its trousers. Sunlight glints off its many cufflinks.

When challenged, it sniffs noselessly, and opens its cloak to look for its fob, revealing a red, felt-lined cavity where its heart should be. Time noted (it's always noon), the fight may begin.

The two jousters take their places, and thunder towards each other. The bejewelled beetle usually runs left at the last second, leaving the charging Knight to barrel into the crowd in confusion.

After much disentangling, the noble Knight will steer around, and approach the Haberdash and its rejoicing steed, the beetle rampant in a triumphal war dance, waving its mandibles in the air.

Believing it has won, the Haberdash blossoms with

smugness, and a gloved hand goes automatically for its snuff box. Fumbling in the opening in its chest, it spills tobacco all over its green silk cloak, empowdering itself into a lurid lokum. It gives a cloth-muffled shriek, and flings the remnants of snuff at the Knight Errand, which splutters and chokes inside its helmet, and falls off its destrier. This farce takes place regularly.

The Knight lies wriggling on its back, a lean metallic turtle, overturned and unable to rise.

The visitor, or prospective resident, may use this as an opportunity to test their levels of empathy.

THE JACKOFALL

Amid the chaos, a gargantuan arachnid clambers over the wall. Splattered with paint, and wearing the remnants of a smock over its manifold limbs, it moves like a hand playing a complicated scherzo.

It brandishes a paintbrush, a pen, a chisel, and a trumpet, and its remaining appendages propel the creature around the piazza, as its eight maddened eyes dart about in a curious mixture of excitement and woe.

Poor Jackofall, master of none!

THE HERALD

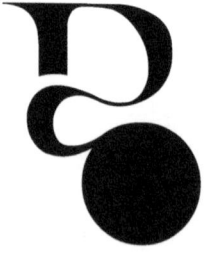owling with ominous purpose towards any new arrival, the Herald takes the form of an enormous broadsheet newspaper, crumpled together like an overgrown tumbleweed.

Captured, the visitor writhes, screeching, as the obituaries page creeps down the back of their neck.

Montcorbier then claps at the ball, and it withdraws with a peevish rustle, orbs itself up again, and bustles off to thwack into the Jackofall, whose spindly, agitated legs entangle with the wriggling newsprint.

The Herald avoided its work by keeping abreast of matters. It lived vicariously through The Times. Reading about them, reporting on them, writing scintillating letters to the editor—it's all one.

Hide from your Vision in the turmoils and trifles of the world, and in the Eternal Carnation you become yesterday's news.

THE MAÑANAS

mitting the roar of a raging fire, deep red sand scours around the globes of the Piazza's central hourglass. Within the maelstrom, the Mañanas lie lax, buffeted to and fro. The coarse particles pour into their open mouths and cake the lashes of their closed eyelids.

The sands perennially flow between the upper and lower chambers, as time did not exist for those who convinced themselves their time would last forever.

Three human statues guard the hourglass: Proud and impassive Gold, aged and gleeful White, and weeping, melancholy Silver.

Montcorbier sometimes squeezes Silver's trembling hand in passing, and there is nothing wrong with this.

THE FUGITIVES

eyond the seething hourglass sprouts a forest of easels. A relative calm surrounds the Fugitives, which dwelled in other artists' art. Within each painting, a lone figure stands and looks around astonished, mesmerised by the painted perfection of its borrowed world.

Sunk within the chalk drawings on the paving stones, there lurks a similar and maudlin tale. Some of the artists who roam inside the sketches are trapped in idyllic lands of mist and beauty. Some adventure forever on high seas. Others traipse eternally off to the ends of the earth, or mourn the deaths of fictional characters, their square a patch of anguish and genuine heartache. Many more wallow in erotica.

Regardless, they are all escape artists.

A face presses against the canvas from the wrong side, stretching through the paint. Its eyeballs bulge with anxiety. All the characters in its chosen world either died or formed romantic arrangements it didn't approve of. The story didn't end the way it wished. Now it wants to leave. Too late! It should have written its own story. If it chose to live in Canon, it has made its nest and can lie and howl in it.

THE WWWEBBED

peaking of which, sometime in the recent history of the city, a sickly and sinister web formed between the spindles of the hourglass and the nearest arcade. Within this sticky monstrosity, the Wwwebbed thrashes and moans. Lightning lances down the tenacious strands, which curl lovingly around the damned artist, which returns the embrace for a moment before the web withdraws, and goes grey and still.

The Wwwebbed frantically attempts to reanimate it. The web lurches to life and endeavours to strangle its prey, which goes limp with relief.

Montcorbier is uncertain as to the meaning of this Carnation. It is comparatively new, and whilst he learns the names of all residents through judicious thefting of the Misdeed, it tells him nothing of the world they came from.

He tries to keep alert to changes beyond the city by interrogating arrivals, and sometimes he updates his lingo and apparel accordingly, but at heart he is still a product of his times. Whatever they were.

He can barely remember now.

THE KNICKERBOCK

eceptively decrepit, the Knicker-bock—an ancient, wiry being—is attached to the Piazza's window shutters by grappling hooks.

Pith-helmeted and khaki-clad, baring its pipe-stained teeth into the non-breeze of the sweltering piazza, the Knickerbock avoided work through anachronistic adventure.

Its bivouac, parked precariously on a balcony, has its ropes and shackles entangled with washing lines.

The Knickerbock sometimes makes a violent leap across the alleyway, sticks a hook into a plant holder, and clings, gecko-like, to the underside of a window ledge.

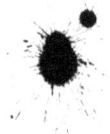

Who lives in these buildings? One might ask.

If one had truly nothing better to do.

Nobody here *lives*, of course. Half these buildings are mere façades. And they are increasingly falling down. The Architect of this shambles of a city cared more for decoration than for substance.

46

Sometimes the street just ends in nothingness.

This has caused Montcorbier some problems after a few drinks at the Vessel!

But it is true the chaos is increasing. A grotesque tumbled off its cornice and nearly decapitated him the other day. It is uncertain which day as they are all the same one. Perhaps it did not tumble. Perhaps it leapt? An investigation is in order.

Although, one can hardly blame it for jumping.

Best to keep an eye open, regardless.

THE CATASTROPHY

he Catastrophy scans the sky with a telescope. Made of yarrow stalks and tea leaves, lashed together with stress and string, the Catastrophy worried about apocalyptic scenarios to avoid its work. It submitted its husk to perpetual health checks and read only the worst news.

Of late it has been looking for impending meteors.

Every few moments, the telescope loses its appeal, and the Catastrophy turns, feverish, towards a collection of bones and runes piled into a small, macabre hill.

THE WHIRLIGIG

ungent fragrance curdles the air, spices stir, scents jostle, and the Whirligig spins by in a mesmerised haze, its voluminous tunic billowing out like ship sails.

It clutches a suitcase rupturing with garish leisure garments, and wears several swords, a pair of clogs, a towering, outlandish hat, and a sarcastically-bestowed flower garland.

The Whirligig found distraction in every country under the sun, that it might shun the inner landscape of its art.

THE RENOVATOR

umming around the buildings like a swarm of industrious bees is the Renovator, a nebulous cloud of sawdust and iron filings. It once buried itself in building projects, hemmed itself in with garden walls, and drowned itself in indoor pond installations. So long as it might make checkerboard tables, its art could wait on a shelf. Once it had built that too.

THE RÉSUMÉ

Jewel-coloured and chortling to itself, a wormlike being creeps across the piazza in a cocoon crafted of various materials and festooned with knick-knacks. It scours the piazza for interesting baubles, and sticks them onto its glittering shell with ponderous complacency.

The Résumé avoided its art by gathering experiences. Until it died. Rather than write its romantic comedy about dubious Mesopotamian copper merchants (or whatever its Heart thought it should be doing), it became instead the manager of an alpine hotel, a pet groomer, a drug smuggler, a bootblack, an escort, a bookie, a ballroom dancer, and in short led a rich and fascinating life.

All, ostensibly, in pursuit of knowledge to render its art authentic—whenever that art eventually occurred.

But its Heart couldn't wait that long.

THE PROSPECTOR

linting in the odious sunlight, a gleaming terrarium rises from the cobbles. White blossoms dance in its imprisoned air. Hunched at a table within, a figure.

The Prospector believed great art only manifested when life was ideal, and thus the stage must be prepared accordingly. It would not begin its work until everything was optimal. First, it needed money, for money brings peace. So, years of establishing an optimal career. Years of searching for the optimal home. Years of searching for the optimal partner.

Eventually, it was ready to begin.

The clouds curled with the optimal amount of beauty. The heady scent of jasmine was in the wind. The pencils were all sharpened. The Prospector was wearing the most comfortable clothing imaginable. A glass of perfectly brewed tea steamed seductively by its hand.

In the courtyard of its optimal domicile, its optimal children frolicked, a charming testament to their progenitor. Its spouse, optimal, prepared the optimal evening meal, and was optimally contented, and not at all desperate to regain their self-identity.

The Prospector was now ready to write THE GREAT BOOK OF OUR TIME. Except—it's dead. A blood clot had found its optimal position in its left anterior descending artery.

In dying, the Prospector damned itself for not beginning just a *tad* earlier.

The Prospector, now Eternally Carnated, has crystallised in lifelike position. On its table the tea yet steams, the pencil is still poised, and the paper remains blank. It will sit there forever, its Vision boiling in its skull. It cannot let it out. It will not flow from its mind, to its hand, to its page. It fumes and frets and thrashes internally against its invisible bindings. But it cannot move. It cannot act. It screams, but cannot scream. The jasmine is optimal.

The City of Lost Intentions

II

THE EMPTY VESSEL

NEGLECT OF ART

PIFFLERS

HE TAVERN IS A CHAOTIC-LOOKING AFFAIR: WOODEN, FLIMSY, AND RAMSHACKLE, WITH DEEP SET STAINED-GLASS WINDOWS TINTED INTERNALLY WITH NICOTINE AND GENERAL FUG.

Though an optimistic few tables are littered around outside, for most of the clientele the noonday sun is a bit *much*. Over the awning, a sign announces, 'Drunk for the Idea, Sober for the Execution', in a style attempting Jugendstil. Needless to say, the Pifflers have never been executed.

THE IDYLL

gainst the sun-warmed tavern wall lounges a being made of flowers, its tulip eyes shaded by a pair of fuchsia spectacles. It exhales a languorous puff of lavender air. Stretching, luxuriant, resplendent in the rays, the indolent Idyll plucks a petunia from its kneecap, opens its daffodil mouth and opines:

'THE POINT OF BEING A POET IS NOT TO WRITE POEMS, BUT TO SEE THE WORLD POETICALLY.'

Montcorbier is prone to kicking the Idyll, which doesn't end well for either of them. If you can imagine a stick insect fighting a wedding bouquet.

THE SLUMMER

From the doorway a leg extrudes like a cricket's limb emerging from the mandible of a lizard which has paused mid-chew in reptilian thought. That the leg is lemon-pastel-panted, and rather insectile to begin with, adds pleasingly to the impression.

The leg belongs to the Slummer. A type of aristo-dabbler who thought that merely falling low enough to consort with riffraff made it bohemian, and therefore a bona fide artist. It wallowed gleefully in its societal ruination and did very little else.

This Carnation is kin to the Sexile, who removed itself to far-flung lands—usually because the near-flung didn't want it—and set up with attractive servants whilst pretending to write villanelles.

The Slummer has passed out across the threshold, acting as a combined doorstop and very unwelcome mat. The oak door thuds against its linen-clad torso with every entry or exit.

THE FROWSY NEST

T he carpet inside is hectic. Violent and nutritious with spilled drinks. Fecund with fungus and fertile with rot. An aged and ageless, decomposing, self-sustaining floorskin, with various humanoid specimens scattered over its virulent surface.

Upon entering the tavern, Montcorbier will bang imperiously on the rickety wall, and the nest of Pifflers will awaken as one monstrous behemoth.

Papers flutter, pipes clatter, squawks emerge, sentences are bitten off, proclamations are strangled, murmurs muffled. In sudden interest, straggled necks crane, and watering yellow eyeballs peer, glistening, through the smoke bank of tobacco. An isolated Mustdash preens itself in profile, twirling its ends. An Entrenched Coat puts its hackles up. A Caveat adjusts itself. Great activity flourishes in the snugs. Red-calloused tentacles cling protectively to pints of shout. Ink-dabbled phalanges twitch. A framed, erotic caricature falls down. Gets up, dusts itself off, and leaves.

The drinks list, pinned to the wall with a bodkin, reads:

SPIRITEDS
Ruminate
Whiskaway
Chagrin
Absent

FOUGHTIFIEDS
Chéri
Starboard
Gingerly Whine

CHEERS
Ail
Shout
Blagger

WHINES
Dread (Hovel)
Fight (Hovel)
Coat do Ruin
Bawd-O
Champ-at-the-Bit

COAT TAILS
Chagrin and Chronic
Whiskaway and Sober
Ruminate and Choke

You may order what you wish, but please note that the tavern is, of late, out of almost everything except dread whine and Absent, which is an unhealthy combination.

Some vital cog is failing somewhere in the normal functioning of the city. A less apathetic Guide would investigate, and perhaps do something about it.

But he is, so he won't. And so forth.

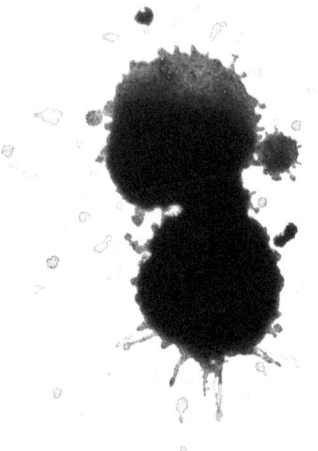

THE BLOODLINER

Bloated and bloviating, a flea in a camel-coloured trench coat has its shiny head bent over the bar in fiendish industry, maxillary palpi twitching with excitement.

It is sketching its family tree upon a napkin, its lavish waistcoat dotted with mustard.

Rather than work upon its art in the present, the Bloodliner found it easier to leap aboard the fame of its ancestors. It spent its days draining the vitality of its listeners to the dregs with tales of its own nobility, told in a drawling voice containing all the ornamental elongation and nasality of an ivory nose pick.

The Bloodliner cares not for you, but it cares intensely for where you've been. And if you're from somewhere nondescript, ergo haven't sprung from anywhere illustrious, then you can fuck off.

THE BLOODSUCKER

*a*ttached to the hump of the Bloodliner is a leech-like creature that preferred to cultivate influential contacts in readiness for its art, rather than actually producing any.

When the Bloodliner illustrates its descent from an ancient artistic genius via pathways unknown to reason, the scrawled mess on the napkin may *look* like a genealogist's headache, but the soused Bloodsucker still lashes its slimy black tail about in encouragement, despite having heard the Bloodliner's fable of origin a thousand times previously.

Bloodsuckers have a mutually beneficial relationship with Bloodliners, and it keeps them both from bothering others.

THE DOGGED

Grumbling on the floor near this unsavoury pair, a small, squat creature slavers with alcoholic froth. A manuscript gripped in its mouth stoppers its perpetual growl, while its overgrown, nicotine-yellow claws skitter on the bare wood, the carpet having been long since shredded. It is tethered to the bar by the remnants of a red woollen scarf wound raggedly round its neck.

In life it had written the same book for fifty years, so it didn't find being Carnated particularly bothersome, there being little distinction between this life and its previous one.

From time to time, it drops the sodden, tooth scored manuscript at its feet and scratches away a comma, but then great apprehension comes over its bestial brain, and it whimpers until a passing soul kindly puts the comma back again.

Occasionally a fellow tavern patron, or Montcorbier in a benevolent mood, might attempt to wrestle the work off the Dogged, only to be savaged by tiny, time-blunted teeth.

THE MADELEINE & FRIEND

ulsome tobacco strand eyebrows wiggle with eloquence, as a creature of self-liquored sponge sits at a table and crumbles itself around with every gesticulation, speaking constantly to nobody in particular.

Its boots leak espresso, its head rises into a spike bearing many impaled receipts, and its mouth is a downturned croissant.

The Madeleine was once a café dweller, overly-fond of reminiscing. It rummages endlessly in a bottomless bowl of olives in front of it, flaky hand independent of its mind. It is surrounded by a veritable mountain of olive pits.

At its feet, the Proustipine—a prickly round forest of smoking, stramonium-scented spines—rootles among the table legs. Finds and eats small pieces of its companion off the floor.

THE REVERED

Woven eyes blink languidly in a crocheted, crimson face as the Revered, body composed entirely of elbow patches, stares sightlessly across the room, lost in a haze of self-admiration.

It smokes constantly, burning little holes in itself. A tiny glass of pale green liqueur sits before it, an oasis in the desert of the Revered's self-absorbed reverie.

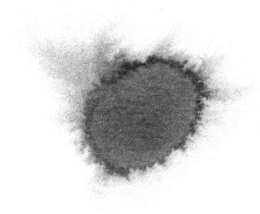

THE HYPERSOPHER

blur of motion like a propeller. Emerging from the blur, sudden flashes. Long, elegant hands! A pipe! A wine glass!

The Hypersopher had been addicted to idle conversation of the hypothetical, quasi-philosophical sort.

(Would you kill one baby or two adults? Would you save one baby or the only copy of Shakespeare's plays? Who would win in a fight between ten babies and Shakespeare only using his left leg? What is your minimum price for eating a piece of human flesh? What if the flesh was Shakespeare's? Etc.)

It whirrs at a high pitch as it flutes forth its theories on moral perfectionism.

THE WINOCERAS

eering from a gloomy great leathery hulk, small watery black eyes fix upon an elephantine bottle rising from its snout in place of a horn. The dark glass glints beneath its cloak of dust.

The Winoceras was overly enamoured of its horn and spent all its time talking about past carousing.

THE MIDWIFE

n the floor between the tables, a writer grapples with their unseen Muse. Twisting and contorting all over the revolting carpet, the writer shrieks, tangling with the chair legs. It rolls under the far table and remains out of sight for a time, weeping. It re-emerges and begins a rigorous enactment of something self-involved and amorous.

Should you be witnessing this? Probably not. But if it will attempt art in public, we must all pay the cost.

THE sQUIRE

 earby, on a small platform, a headless tweed suit is giving a poetry recital. It wears a burgundy bow tie around its absent neck, and its marigold yellow gloves weave in graceful, theatrical gestures as its hollow, melodious voice drifts throughout the tavern.

It has only three poems, but it has bound them nicely, on handmade, heavyweight paper, with many epigraphs and dedications.

Alas, everything it says is in a private headless suit language, which only the sQuire understands. This makes selling chapbooks somewhat strenuous.

Recently, Montcorbier (for reasons), launched himself at the sQuire and attempted to get it into a headlock. Suffice to say, this failed, and the disgruntled Guide simply latched the sQuire's cufflinks together behind its back, leaving it to flounder around on stage like a herringbone fish, expelling a stream of indignant nonsense.

Montcorbier's composure of late is, admittedly, troublesome and uppity, but it's to be expected, given his intolerable situation.

THE HOARY ELD

I n the far corner a gaunt tortoise draped in a voluminous fur shawl watches on with a venomous glare. Its nictitating membrane drags, viscid, across its gristly eyeballs from behind an awkwardly positioned pince nez.

It knows you were not invited.

THE BOUNDER

obbing up and down on a barstool, sulfur head crest blown in agitation, is the Bounder, enraged over its extensive bar tab. The size of a toddler, its talons curl, elegant and threatening, around the seat, as it fixes its victims with its tiny, mad eye.

The Bounder created scandals and intrigues to avoid its work, and spent most of its time dealing with the fallout, instead of dealing with its Vision.

It is meant to be in the Piazza with the rest of the Prevaricators, but, being a larrikin, it has taken liberties.

THE KALEIDOQUOTE

oosely humanoid, a cluster of plastic beads slouches against the bar. Every movement it makes shifts the beads into a unique pattern.

Arabesques, starbursts, indeterminate squiggly things. With each way they tilt, a new dazzling array.

All lovely and pointless. Self-mesmerising. The Kaleidoquote turns a fetching pink and purple triangular shape, and jostles contentedly.

If someone, no-one in particular, but say Montcorbier, reaches for a bottle behind the counter and puts his hand through the Kaleidoquote, it will splutter in astonishment and pop into a scatter of iridescence and garishness which proceeds to roll under the armchairs and pinball around the floor.

Someone always sweeps it up, eventually.

It re-forms within the hour.

THE BILLBORING

The Billboring stands booming about its work, whirling around like a weathervane in high wind. Resembling a movie marquee on opening night, it is a two-dimensional artist, but very well lit.

One of its bulbs has blown. It will have it replaced within the hour. After all, it is very well connected.

THE ALLEGONY

lat, glazed, covered in oil paint and folded into a triptych, the Allegony broods by the fire. It sketched grandiose, allegorical pictures on napkins and table tops, but then became crushingly aware of how long it would take to create these marvels, so sank into despondency and painted nothing.

THE BLETTED MEDLY

ccompanying the Allegony is the Bletted Medly. A stranded minstrel with a face like a wrinkled apple, it plays its lute, hums a few heartbreaking bars, then lapses into daydreams about fame, interviewing itself.

By this point in proceedings, the visitor—possibly in a foetal position—is often a tad overstimulated, having been besieged by a cavalcade of sights and smells whilst stuck in the company of a sarcastic fop and a parade of monsters, and may try reasoning with the Guide, and suggest that rather than go any further in this unsettling city, it would be best, perhaps, to remain a while in the tavern.

Montcorbier would not normally be adverse to this, but he is on the clock (a complicated procedure in a city of repeating days), and moreover has conducted this tour times numberless, and is therefore immune to any watery-eyed appeals from prospective residents.

So where to now?

Somewhere a little less wholesome.

Exit through the back door, out into the endless noonlight.

III

THE GILDED GROTTO

INFIDELITY TOWARDS ART

PANBACCHANALS

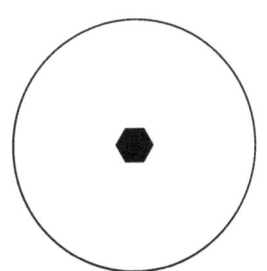

N THE FAR SIDE OF A CRAMPED, DIRTY COURTYARD, TWO MASSIVE GOLDEN DOORS SHINE, OBSCENE AMIDST THE MURK.

A red carpet slithers over the general filth on the cobbles, intersected by a frayed, gold-tasselled rope which marks out where the clientele should wait, if they had any manners.

Inside, a stupendous open maw of a gold cave roars and gorges, the glistening walls pockmarked with plush alcoves and grottoes, cushioned with silks and matted furs drenched in the juices of all manner of activities. Moist, stifling, overripe scents breed with suffocating musks, yielding fleshy odours of animal or intimate origin. Huge, rough-cut jewels lie strewn across tarnished silverware, commingling with rotten grapes, salted herrings, loose saffron, baroque pearls, and roast pigs' trotters. Haunches of smoked meat hang from the gilded ceiling, gather moisture and drip interesting liquids down between the chandeliers.

The battered gold floor, worn by the staggering passage of countless reprobates, has fruit pulp trodden into the grooves like a revolting grout.

In the centre of the room, a golden fountain holds three naked shining figures entwined desirously around a serpent. Six inter-caressing hands grasp its sinuous neck, and its tail loops the basin's rim.

A sequence of fluids pour warmly forth from its tapered mouth in successive squirts: a cascade of chocolate gives way to one of truffle oil, of cream, of pomegranate juice, of oyster sauce, then a deluge of pungent balsamic reduction, basting the threesome in a glutinous curdle of condiments.

It's all rather sticky.

The Panbacchanals sold their Muse down the river for a brief cruise on a luxury boat. Eventually, the vessel struck the sandbanks, and their talents turned to cannibalism.

In short, if you intend to sail the crystal ship, you must never cease to sound.

Their crime was infidelity, seduction by something other than their art, a fascination that pulled them away from their labours. You must fight this undertow, should it begin to pluck at you, threatening to drag you under, or your Vision will never see the light of day.

For the Heart is easily slighted and demands faithfulness. That the artist obey no other commands.

Except the Guide's, when touring his city.

Do what he says or he will become insufferable.

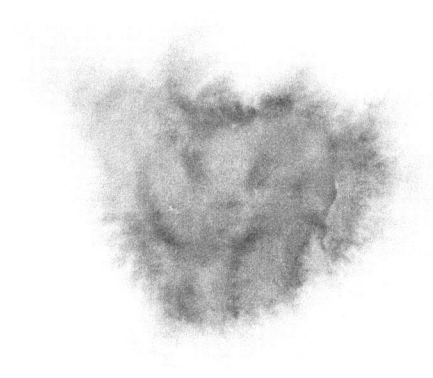

THE GLUTTON

efore a bulging barrel squatting like an ominous, bloated god supervising sacrificial festivities, a fattened monk, a well-dressed leper, and a faun with blackened eyes dance the gavotte.

A bawdy feast rollicks away at a low table by a fire, the revellers raising glasses and basking in the refracted rays of flame and the scent of toasted Glutton.

Composed of crackling, the Glutton spins slowly on a spit. It wallows obliviously in the grease, sunk in the sun of its pleasure as it devours itself. Eventually it bursts into flames and has to be doused in ale by its companions.

THE SKALDED

great slab of a woeful Viking hulks nearby at the golden bar, clutching a polished horn. Its wrinkle-rimmed, weary and watery red eyes seem to look towards Ragnarök. Once it was a skald, the toast of its village. But it fell into the mead, finding the spirits that dwelled within more entertaining than the roasted bores without. Eventually it could no longer both sing *and* swim, so sank, to settle its lyre amongst the lees. It had presumed it was in Valhalla, and remains rather confused about its fellow Einherjar.

THE DON WAN

he Don Wan powders itself endlessly. Indeed it is made almost entirely from powder and pomade. Its bejewelled wax fingers squeak as it repeatedly laces, unlaces, and re-laces its various bits of suffocating apparel. It dislocates an arm to tighten its corset, straighten its stockings, and reapply its beauty spots.

The Don Wan spent its days beautifying itself for its lovers. All its energies flowed towards perfecting its instrument of wooing—itself.

Unlike the Haberdash, who hid in finery out of fear, the Don Wan was in love with courtship for the sake of it. It pushed its art off its plinth and stuck a mirror there. It was unfaithful to its Vision whenever there was a fetching face to admire, or a noble heart to win.

Which was constantly.

THE TASTELESS FEASTERS

ut deep into the golden walls is an oversize white marble triclinium, cushioned with goose down covered in raw, scarlet silk, in a scene reminiscent of a Roman banquet hall.

Decadence lies strewn across the lounges as though detritus left by a dissipating and dissipated tide. Jaundiced figures loll in stained, encrusted togas, picking with apathy through the ruins of a feast.

The centrepiece is a Purostfilark: larks' tongues, stuffed inside a fish fed on the flesh of learned slaves, stuffed inside an ostrich, stuffed inside a Purpose, displayed on a large platter.

At the core of this monstrosity, nestled appallingly among the tongues, was meant to lie the bluebird of happiness, but mercifully it got away in time.

None of the Tasteless Feasters ever ate that far anyway, being, by then, considerably and rightfully ill.

Gelatinous and gleaming, translucent glacé fruit Carnations crawl stickily around the remains. Toffee plasters their features and snaps and crackles in their joints. A rock-sugar beast sits on a velvet pillow, licking itself with a sparkling tongue.

All the surrounding gold lends the tableau the air of a Pharaonic tomb, the heavy opulence merely gilding death.

Before the triclinium, the golden floor buckles and gives way to a crevice, a yawning gorge filled with teeth and strings of slaver. Into the monstrous mouth pour endless delicacies from a cornucopia overhead.

Do watch where you step.

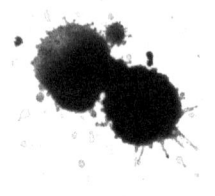

THE SOMMELIER

 n the far side of this ghastly pit, waiters weave around tables in a serpentine dance. Mirrors amplify the waiters until the whole resembles a seething wall of servile snakes, all attending to an enormous nose perched atop a spindly, black-suited body sitting folded in upon a delicate gold chair.

Its nostrils, each the size of a human head, flare splendidly, their shells glowing in the light. A tiny hand holds a small glass of wine beneath these olfactory caves, which quiver as they draw in the bouquet, fine hairs stirring in the gentle breeze.

The Sommelier, cheating on its book, is engaged in tasting every wine under the sun. Or rather, every wine in the cellars.

A considerable amount, owing to the Architect possessing an appreciation for the grape, and thus equipping the city with a substantial number of bottles. Which is fortunate for Montcorbier and his dismal and eternal tippling habits.

Deep from the golden bowels of the cellar emerges a further stream of scuttling waiters, each bearing a bottle before them like a lantern.

Over the course of the never-ending evening, they show the Sommelier the entire contents of the vinous catacombs.

To each of the bottles it gives a sniff, in both senses, and gestures to the unflagging waiters to begin again. Indeed, they have never stopped. The wine is on a perpetual lemniscate of display.

THE BIJOUFLY

At the next table, a ginormous butterfly, burdened by jewellery, struggles to rise. Brilliant ropes of gold and turquoise loop around its narrow neck, its velvet wings pulsing frantically. It flutters its feelers at a giant crab sitting on a platter before it, claws bound with pearl necklaces, similarly fighting to stand under a shell of faceted tourmaline. Both are doomed by the weight of luxury they sought to the detriment of their homespun art.

THE VANITAS

unched in a corner, the skeletal Vanitas stitches itself a cloak from feathers plucked from a nearby peacock, weaving them together with gold and silver thread.

The peacock is magnificent, and knows it. Each iridescent, self-renewing feather is gorgeous, its colours intricately blended.

The Vanitas warded off death with beauty. It garbed itself in finery in rebellion against mortality and meaninglessness, defiance in the face of a godless universe. Glitter hurled at death, even if death will dodge.

But alas, it cloaked only itself and left its Vision bare, thus the Vanitas cowers under a gilded shawl forever.

THE sCOWL

Behind this ad hoc tailor stands an ox skeleton in a humble, dirt-brown wool cloak of simple design.

The sCowl was a Prevaricator which had chosen to avoid its art by being a moralising prig. No-one knows how the killjoy got into the Grotto. If it is possible for an ox skull to look disapproving, this one does.

It saves most of its disapproval for Montcorbier, whenever he swans into its empty eye-socket-line.

In this case, the sCowl is right to disapprove.

THE EPICUREAN

Browsing in the radicchio foliage by the fountain is a long creature made almost entirely of toothpicks and garnishes.

Its head is a small triangle of brie, and its eyes are two stuffed olives encircled by boquerone eyelids.

Its proboscis is stuck in a cocktail and a ruff of fennel sprouts charmingly around its breadstick neck.

The Guide has a terrible habit of plucking bits off the Epicurean to pick his teeth, despite never eating anything. Although he will say it was only once, and to cheer up a particularly sombre poet.

THE CARNABARET

verything glisters in the Carnabaret. When you enter the shimmering grotto, you receive a handful of spangles flung in the face so you match the décor, and the emcee will solemnly press a gold star sticker to your forehead.

A throng of oscillating tassels and rampant codpieces surrounds you, as creatures formed entirely from the intricate bits of human anatomy gyrate and writhe, gold dust clumping uncomfortably in their moist hollows and encrusting their protuberances.

On stage, orifices hovering in the air swallow other orifices, fleshy trumpets blossom, then curl back and inwards, resembling a sort of carnal Klein bottle, and the Möbius Striptease, a great doughy stretch of blushing flesh, pulls apart and contorts.

No singular figure can be identified, only a nebulous mass of polymorphous perversity.

In the audience, engorged and straining creatures made of skin and veins sit at small tables and throb at one another. The centrepiece of each table is a seedy, lurid tropical flower, from which emanates a rich, fermented cloud of spores when prodded or otherwise interfered with.

Try not to interfere with it.

Casketloads of animate meat pack every corner of the platform. A desultory, pleasureless orgy is taking place in a vat of grapes.

The visitor would be advised not to drink the house wine.

THE ILLUMINED

isps of honeyed smoke caress a burgundy drape concealing a hollow at the back of the Carnabaret, pooling around the puddle of velvet piled on the floor, and drifting on lazily.

Montcorbier will peel back the edge of the curtain and slip through like a dissipated sylph, the smoke curling out in a languid huff behind him.

Follow the villain.

First you creep, blind, through the wall of scented haze, your eyes watering, then you enter a womblike darkness, lit only by a pulsing treacle glow.

As the throbbing light grows stronger, you will behold a chamber of polished amber, supported by malachite columns. Creatures lie trapped within the resin, gaunt forms and faces contorted in eternal illumination.

Another fountain gurgles in this grotto. Its three bronze basins rise in diminishing size, ornamented with arabesques. Over the rims, absinthe and cognac, sherry and chartreuse, erguotou and ouzo, waterfall down in intoxicating turn.

At the top of the whole ensemble sits the hunched, wearied and shady-looking Bacchanal, who looks to have a splitting headache, pouring endlessly from a bottomless amphora.

The air is cloying and heady with scents. A mingling of opium, fever sweat, cannabis, decaying agarwood, and apathy. Each breath drags a caravanserai of odours into the lungs.

Spindly glass beings, arrayed delicately upon chaise longues, seem assembled from a chemist's collection of pipettes, flasks, decanters, and distilling paraphernalia. Brightly coloured smoke curls within the chambers of their transparent limbs.

A winged, slothlike entity hangs from the ceiling, fairy-green eyes lit up like railway lanterns. A long plumed individual rolls along a rug, wisping off at the extremities, whilst red vapours coil in its neighbour's translucent abdomen, spiralling up to extrude from its multiple mouthpieces.

A crystal exoskeleton shines in the gloom, head filled with light. Another resembles a peeled mandarin, glossy flesh glutinous and luminous, swollen to near bursting as its veins perpetually boil with tincture.

As the smoke colours change, so the mood drifts from melancholy, to epiphany, rapture, disenchantment, dismay, despondency, and back to melancholy.

The artist's Vision begins to blur as the days flicker,

and eventually shudders to nothingness.

A minute in the grotto and an hour passes outside, and doesn't look in.

Montcorbier has tried ceaselessly to get the Illumined to impart their wisdom, but bupkis, to use a word he has recently learned from a visitor.

The problem with those in perpetual states of enlightenment is they are often too stupefied by it to enlighten anyone else.

THE INTELLECTUAL HEDONISTS

loating within a vast golden aviary entwined with tropical blooms and fruit-laden vines, clouds of Flutterbys, some bold and bright, others ethereal, trail their swallow-tails after them like shredded cathedral veils.

The hummingbirdesque Sampler moves with geometric precision around the cage, sticking its pointy tongue into all the flowers.

Nearby, claws fixed to a bough, a tall, white Mockatoo hangs upside down, stripping clusters of grapes from the canopy. It shrieks and chatters content-edly to itself, pointlessly destroying great swathes of foliage.

Although the method of their madness seems the same, the Intellectual Hedonists within the aviary are distinct from their fellow hobbyists in the piazza (such as the Jackofall and the Résumé) in that their distraction was not a ploy to escape their art, they were, instead, genuinely lured away, beguiled by wind patterns, labyrinths, languages, code-cracking, crosswords, and the music of the spheres.

Seduced by intellectual puzzles in lieu of puzzling out their Vision. Anything that lit up the branches of their brain with delight.

Playing cards litter the floor of the cage amidst fallen grapes and multi-coloured feathers. Suits and evening dresses filled with more playing cards sit at rickety tables, staring at the hand they dealt themselves, each face a fake silver coin.

THE GAMBIT

lone at a corner table of the aviary, a highly polished ivory horse's head jammed into a bugle-beaded flapper dress is engrossed in a game of chess with itself. After every move it changes colour, from black to white or white to black, then spins the board to avoid the inconvenience of changing sides. Oleaginous mist from the humid air gathers around its carved mane and seeps down to stain the silk of its outfit.

Why a Knight, and not some other figure? Who decides such matters?

Not the Architect. Not for a long time.

But why, if self-Carnated as a chess piece, would the Gambit not choose to be a Queen or King?

Montcorbier quite understands not wanting to be a King. Functionally hobbled, largely ornamental, and everyone wants to kill you. Your death is the aim of the game. But better a King than a pawn, he supposes. At least you get a nice hat. If he were a monarch, the first thing he'd do is demand a nice hat. Then he'd make the sun set on this unbearable city.

But that is neither here nor there.

THE BORROWER BIRD

ccasionally, a caw breaks from the cage ceiling, and a great flash of dark wings swoops past. Talons grab for anything dangling about your person, and the feathered menace returns to its nest, a complex kingdom built at cage-crown, garlanded with gewgaws and arbitrary objects of interest:

Bronze fibulae, a snake-charmer's reed flute, a gong, a dowsing stick, snatches of brocade, cartographical instruments, a small embroidered decorative camel, and now, after one of Montcorbier's recent visits, a rather shabby wineskin.

The Borrower Bird will carefully tuck its new acquisition underneath an astrolabe, and preen its glossy black feathers, which seem overlain with rainbow iridescence as though they had been dipped in oil.

Montcorbier would *like* to dip it in oil.

One of the problems with being the only self-aware inhabitant of a realm of eternal Carnations, is that all agreements, deals sealed, conversations of note, etcetera, are swiftly forgotten by the other beings involved in them.

Whilst this gives Montcorbier something of an

advantage, insofar as his dismal behaviour is likewise forgotten, it also means he has to repeatedly remind the Carnations that he is in fact vital to this whole catastrophe and is therefore not to be eaten, brutalised, threatened, lied to, or (in the case of the Borrower Bird) thieved from. For it may be the Borrower Bird, but it is yet to give anything back.

Possibly, as an individual prone to collecting garments, jargon and shiny objects—either stolen from visiting artists over the centuries, or snitched from the dressing rooms of the H'Auditorium—Montcorbier feels insulted to be bested at the practice of illegitimate acquisition.

And the wretch is expanding its talents.

Last time, the feathered miscreant hopped over to the latch on the cage and unhooked it with its claw. An awful pause followed. The bird raised its shoulders into an oily black mound. A hovering, malignant wet mop, which then launched itself towards the Don Wan and the miserable Skalded, soaring like an animated Stygian tablecloth over the Grotto.

The Don Wan flapped at the mighty avian terror with one lace glove, eyes appalled. The Skalded flung its horn. Mead-drenched, the Borrower Bird eyed both offerings, chose neither, and shied off to land at the base of the bulging wine barrel, and stabbed its beak into the cork.

With a triumphal flutter, and a reverberating comical POP!—it pulled the bung from the barrel. Gallons of wine roared forth in a torrent of burgundy.

Chaos reigned as the flow became gargantuan.

It swept up the tables, flooded the golden hall, with shrieks and gurgles filling the air, and cresting high, the Bacchanal rode the waves delightedly in its copper fountain basin, headache forgotten.

In a final, contemptuous gush, the stream flushed all the Carnations and Montcorbier out the double doors into the street, to lie upon the cobbles like beached lampreys, wine-soaked and steaming unpleasantly in the sun.

And that's enough of that.

.

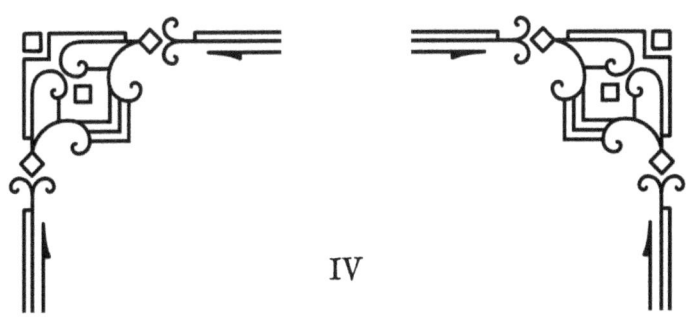

IV

THE H'AUDITORIUM

DIMINISHMENT OF ART

Pasquinades

Entering the theatre is like walking into a mouth. A decadent, rich, plush red velvet one, filled with gold teeth and horseshoe braces.

Mercifully free of gum disease, or syphilis, but frankly too full of candles and rococo ornaments for this image to work.

Let us abandon it.

A triple mezzanine, gilded and scalloped, towers ominously over the pit. From the gods, mindless chatter drifts down like ash.

Peanut shells also pelt down, but only rarely.

The decorations are wealthy and exquisite, and so is the audience. Since, as in life, their only reason for going to the theatre was to make a social impression, they have forgone the need for actual attendance, and simply sent their outfits to hell instead.

Headless suits lounge louchely, ballgowns bustle, silk qipaos slither decorously among the tuxedos, jostling occasionally with a hátíðarbúningur, whilst furs slink, and kilts jaunt saucily down the aisles.

Fascinators, hovering on nothingness, pierce upwards like the spines of a late-Jurassic monster, glued with sprays of gilded plumes, wrested warm from the corpse of some rare, inedible bird.

Trilbies and Homburgs hobnob silently with each other amidst Eau de Colognic clouds, artificial gemstones glittering with unwholesome light in the scented haze.

For this sartorial clanjamfry is choked with perfumes, which is just as well, since the cloistered materials have, over the centuries, acquired a high, almost violent reek of sweat, produced in fear of falling out of fashion.

We all need love, but the attention seeking Pasquinade needed love to such a degree that it sacrificed it Vision in exchange. It whittled it down into a more pleasing form, because the Heart's Vision is sometimes a peculiar thing, of limited appeal, and loved by no-one else.

The Pasquinade diminished its art so it would fit within an acceptable vista. It rounded the corners of its square peg and trimmed the thorns from its rose. Everything left was perfectly palatable. But it had no spice. No colour. No sting. No bite.

If pressed, Montcorbier might say, diffidently:

'If you take your Heart's great Vision, the thing you would wish to walk upon the earth in your absence, and because it walks out of beat with the times you hobble it so that it walks in step, then by your Heart's admittedly unfair dictate you are a wretch, and will be Carnated here in eternal mockery.'

How he knows this with such certitude is a matter of conjecture, but rest assured, he is an unfortunate expert on the topic.

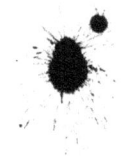

THE BOOTLICKS

ittle Bootlicks, the size of Chihuahuas, sit dribbling upon the empty finery, whose bejewelled hollow-glove fingers tangle in their perfumed ringlets. Their ruffs, accordioned pages of etiquette books, flare out like those of frill-necked lizards.

The Bootlicks strived only to keep in favour and please the court of contemporaneity, ignoring the wilder demands of their Hearts.

THE CHIMPIONED

Upon the stage, a chimpanzee dressed in a tiny, diamond-checked suit, perched on a unicycle, weaves unsteadily around an array of obstacles: a bottle of a popular type of sparkling water, a tin of famous pomade, an upsetting-looking exercise device ...

The Chimpioned had been a brilliant artist who had somehow become a brand ambassador. This would not, in and of itself, have been an issue, had the Chimpioned not deflated its muse by using its breath for puff pieces.

THE MOCKAQUE

bove, the Mockaque, in a richly embroidered, paint-splattered clown costume, scampers up the curtain, swings from the lights and becomes entangled in the overhead rigging. It hoots in alarm, then falls, landing in a large cream pie.

There is compensation for its dirtied fur and injured pride in the ample pay of the society circle for whom it performed its society-circular plays.

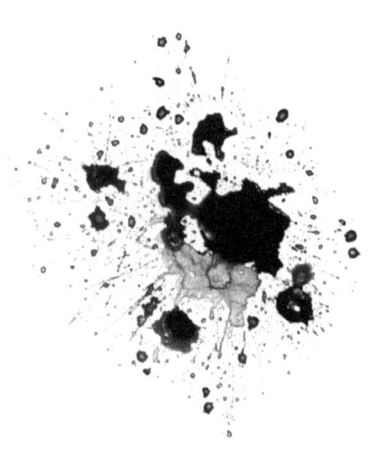

THE VAUDEVILLAINS

audeville churns out endlessly. Buffoons, once artists capable of great subtlety, run through shonky comedic routines, and balance on lurid circus balls, their grease-painted masks of mirth cracking as they gurn, while Pantomimics stitched inside two-dimensional caricatures of themselves fight to escape their mimetic prison.

Rapture greets their panicked bumbling around the stage, buffets of applause from the handless audience as they flap their gloves and sleeves together thundering like a thousand beaten rugs on a windy day.

Tragedians in revealing dress, anxious sweat cutting tracks through the rouge, contort themselves into amusing or obscene shapes, their Shakespearean souls internally howling in protest from the turrets of Elsinore. Every so often, a Tragedian runs naked from wing to wing, to wolf whistles.

THE GENUFLECT

eafening, a wave of admiration sweeps over the Genuflect as it bows repeatedly from the stage. Composed entirely of teary-eyed gratitude, its liquid brow quavers under the onslaught of adoration, and rivulets of moisture wander down its water-filled cheeks. The mask of pleasure it wetly wears has long grown pained and fearful, and its whole physiognomy has begun to dissolve, yet it relentlessly bows, and bows. Its jellied spine quakes.

A lull, and another wave of admiration approaches. The air darkens and rustles as hats hurtle skyward in adulation. The Genuflect murmurs thanks, and barely keeps its sickly, flaccid smile from slipping.

THE LIMELIGHT

kyward from the Genuflect, a haunting spectre hangs. A blue and swollen moon, cavernous-eyed and sheening, utmost despair on its luminous face. In life, the Limelight sought constant attention at cost to its work, and now it can never turn its face away from the appreciative crowd.

THE ORCHESTRATORS

The Orchestrators, twisted but elegant notes, sit dully in the pit before the stage. Strings cut, winds muffled. Some gaze sourly at the performance, some mournfully at the audience.

The conductor, a treble clef, sits upon a drum, its curly head held in its hands. Overcome, it shudders with tears.

The violinist, sans violin, flutters hopeless fingers. They quiver like small wings about to take flight.

A pantomime horse falls over on stage and frenziedly kicks itself apart to the sound of a kazoo. The two parts of the horse then fight with each other, as outlandish demons flood the stage and are struck down by a gormless patriotic figure draped in an enormous flag.

The rear of the horse falls off the stage and topples onto the weeping conductor.

Applause erupts again.

THE HATCHETJOB

Spinning, roaring, above the absent heads of the crowd is the Hatchetjob, which murdered others' works in their infancy to settle private scores and gain a cruel but powerful readership.

The blunt axe of its face causes occasional, unintentional injuries, and the velvet-lined box that once bought its loyalty has long since been chopped to splinters.

THE ADULTERATORS

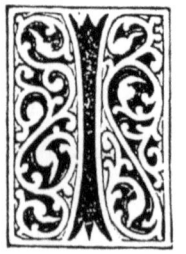n what Montcorbier regards as a spectacularly cruel twist of the punitive knife, the Adulterators run the interval bar.

Made of spun sugar, they turn anything unusual or complex into a cloying wish-wash of marketable insubstantiality.

One adds pink creaming soda to a glass of single malt. A bottle of Châteauneuf-du-Pape is upended into a boiling pot of mulled wine. Benign confusion holds sway over the sugar-drugged clientele, while filaments of fairy floss float in the treacly air, and the dancing Tragedians form a human snake up the aisles.

THE TURNAWAYSTYLE

urking at the backstage door and manipulating a clipboard is the Turnawaystyle.

It wears a yellow carnation—the usual signifier the bearer is part of the machinery of the city—and its many arms spin with agitation as it eyes the potential intruder with blistering hostility, looking them up and down (though given its diminutive stature, rather more up), and snapping demands for lanyards.

Montcorbier does not need a lanyard, as he reminds the Turnawaystyle daily.

He has the keys to this fiasco.

He goes where he pleases.

THE COURTIERS

Stretching out along the Corridor of Cajolery leading to the dressing rooms, a gauntlet of prostrate Courtiers form a snake against both walls.

Each specimen has its satin cloak slotted over the head of the one behind and its teeth sunk into the posterior of its forward fellow, fitting together like the scales of a pangolin.

Between the two rows, cluttering the corridor, loose Courtiers crawl, leaping feverishly at the guests like bejewelled fleas.

Brace yourself. Batten the hatches.

The visitor must inch down the corridor, lifting their legs heronishly high to avoid the layer of grovelling beneath. Otherwise, a silken glove will creep out, tentative, and grasp them by the ankle.

Upon the floor, the musty, huddled mob will edge closer, gearing up to gesticulate, beginning to work up to a soliloquy. A sequinned hand closes upon a stage sword. A bulging oyster of an eye gleams, preparing to manufacture tears.

An audience! Only small, alas.

But still! Enough!

Several of them begin to rise …

Beat them down!

They will cling to your boots and howl impressively. One will begin a sort of ululating wail. Several scream and faint.

Montcorbier will cry: 'O for Melpomene's sake!'

Amid the hullabaloo, the Royal Pass sweeps up the narrow corridor, pressing everybody against the walls. It is two-dimensional and flimsy, so no real harm occurs.

In its wake it leaves a welcome calm as the Courtiers bond in their shared loathing of the upstart.

THE IMPRESSIONABLE

mitting a soft, sucking sound, a wet clay figure lollops at the end of the corridor. If you are foolish enough to go near, it flattens itself and wraps anxiously around you.

If silence ensues, as it invariably will when one is cloaked in clay, it takes this for approval. Satisfied, it peels off with an intaglio cast of your appalled face.

The Impressionable is very clingy.

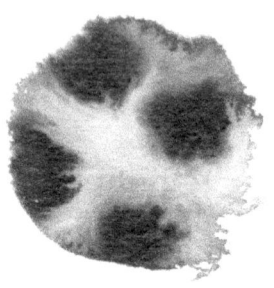

THE BON MOT

utside the dressing room door lurks the Bon Mot. It is a charming figure in its shiny foil-covered tube, its body shimmering beneath a scrunched paper head, long ribbon arms waving. Ribbon legs emerge from its pouffed paper skirt.

Inside its hollow chest, a witticism rattles, tied to a whimsical toy. Protruding from top and bottom of its cylindrical torso are strips impregnated with silver fulminate. Hourly, it feels compelled to grasp these and yank itself apart with a bang.

The witticism tumbles out, is idly read by a passer-by, sniggered over, then is crumpled up and thrown away.

The Bon Mot is in constant anguish over this indifference. Yet still it pieces itself together and manufactures more witticisms. Endlessly. For years. Its art transformed into a trinket.

Its Heart was not amused.

THE TYPECASTS

n the dressing room, great mechanical arms equipped with brushes and sponges paint a row of artists cowering before the gleaming mirrors. Metal pincers grasp and hold them in position. Cogs and gears whirl and click. Faces tragic, sensitive, haughty, woebegone, brutal, whimsical: all are given one mask for all time. Their most popular, best-beloved one, which they despise.

Once released, the Typecasts erupt in hysterics. They rub and claw at their enforced make-up, but nothing removes their designated role.

Some have been re-faced with so many layers of paint they have begun to peel off in parts. Great crags of illusion tear and thud onto the talc-dusted floor.

Their old selves, caught inside the mirror, watch in horror.

THE SPINNING JENNY

hirring in the darkness of a corner, the Spinning Jenny spins itself like a hank of wool onto the wheel and spindle of its industry, of which it had become a product. It screams as it is drawn into a thread.

THE WORLD'S PARAMOUR

very so often, down by the front of the stage, a sacrifice takes place. A crowned, golden statue, the World's Paramour, is thrown off the footlights into the feverish arms of Idolaters, which shriek with the sheer beauty of their idol. Their lustful cries rise as the terrified figure tumbles around, slavered over from every angle.

A hundred plastic effigies of the Paramour are passed sweatily around the crowd. Manufactured for a pittance and sold for a fortune. The Idolaters claw them to pieces in adoration. This done, they claw the Paramour itself. Removing the crown from the remnants of the old World's Paramour, they place it on the apprehensive head of another golden figure, plucked without warning from the ether.

The new Paramour escapes the clawing and is merely licked to death.

THE FROTH & BABBLE

eanwhile, in the mezzanine, a nebulous being crests over the boxes. Boos and applause buffet the Froth and Babble, a Carnation sustained solely by controversy. Eventually its flimsy shape breaks apart and spreads like gossamer across the empty eveningwear, to re-form quietly in a corner.

High above, the Windsock, who altered its work to follow trends, is blustering in the gale of activity.

THE PLAYWRONG

owed over a small table in the wings, a transparent, iridescent Playwrong writes frenziedly on blank pieces of paper, a glint of cold fear in its eye. The words appear briefly, then vanish like disappearing ink. Anything that is not a popular trope can no longer make the cut.

THE PROFLIGATE

I n a cloud of gypsum dust, the Profligate, another wings-dweller, is reproducing itself in dwindling quality, wearing its substance too thin.

Each of its faces is becoming less and less distinct. Rough-edged seams are showing, plaster torsos fill with air-bubbles. The Profligate replicates loudly around you, hollering: 'Twelve plays a year! Twenty gallery openings! One hundred and eight entrancing folksongs!'

THE VOLUBUBBLE

aid by the word, the Volububble spews forth verbosity in great spouts of lilac foam. The word-suds dry into ornate and fanciful sculptures, fragile as meringues.

Occasionally an identical version of the Volububble spawns from the froth, and wrenches itself away from its progenitor. Its old self left vacant, the soul having moved on, soon falls and shatters among the shards of toppled verbiage.

THE SHUSHERS

Clad in yellow carnations, the Shushers wearily clear away the fragments of purple prose. One mutters as it sweeps a particularly effusive outpouring into a sack, along with the drifting sugary gauze from the Adulterators which has spread in a sickening web throughout the theatre.

THE RHUBARB

Watching all the hullabaloo is the resident extra, a large stalk of rhubarb, its toffee-red face shining with condensation under its overhanging leaf. It is a lonely fellow, and you may speak to it, but it can only say rhubarb in return. But it says so with urgency, with appeal:

'*Rhubarb*, rhubarb rhubarb, *rhubarb* rhubarb, rhubarb!'

When eventually, as it must, your focus drifts, the Rhubarb burbles a final 'Rhubarb' and goes sadly away.

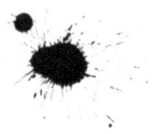

Something unexpected happened recently, on one of Montcorbier's regular tours, a dazed and mildly terrified arrival in tow.

The Saxophant—a collection of wind instruments soldered together into one ungainly physique—emerged from the wings, and fluted:

'The Author of the tragedy is here! The Author! The Author!'

The crowd of clothing rustled excitedly, roused momentarily from torpor.

A gust of greasepaint-scented air, and the lightweight pantomime actors blew away like dandelion seeds, settling in the lighting overhead, and drifting over the audience.

The Limelight held its luminous breath.

Nothing.

Silence stretched out and was abruptly stabbed by a trumpet heralding—

More silence.

The dandelion actors slowly eddied, heavied by disappointment, to the floor.

But who is this Author?

A scoundrel, certainly. They usually are.

It is strange, regardless.

They aren't supposed to know.

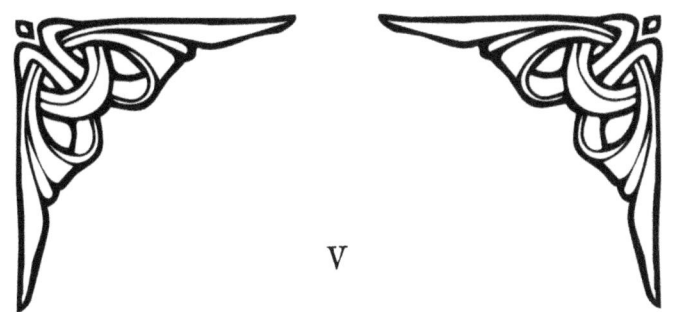

V

THE TEMPLE OF FO-ELPMET-EHT

CONTORTION OF ART

PERIWINKLERS

L OFTY AND FRAGILE, A NON-EUCLIDEAN STRUCTURE RISES IN A CLEAR, WHITE LIGHT. Carved out of brittle ivory, its slender limbs and branches support a lustrous mother-of-pearl shell, and willowy columns recede around the curve into darkness. Seen from above, the shape resembles an ammonite, a perfect mathematical spiral.

Yet there is something uncanny in its perspective which hurts the eye to look at, as though insulted by some visual trickery.

If you approach from the front, however, which is more usual, you are spared this logical indignity.

The inhabitants of this enchanted temple, where even the water in the fountains flows backwards, are the Periwinklers; Carnations which took refuge from their Vision in pedantry, contortion, solipsism, and obscurity, or at least lost their way in them.

They had been artists who made sculptures of triangular relationships in 17th-century jácaras using the symbolism of agricultural propaganda produced in years of high rainfall. Allegorists who wrote allegories about allegorists writing allegories. Writers who classified artistic foibles into various levels of hell. That sort of thing. Some did this deliberately to be unfathomable, out of pride. Others had simply wandered so far inside the labyrinth, taking with them their ball of twine, that they forgot the outside world. Some sought the Minotaur of truth, others fled a spectre that bore their form. Regardless, all became horribly lost. This wouldn't have mattered, obviously, Montcorbier will be at pains to point out, if tortuous, filigreed mayhem had been their *intent*. If you wish to craft a work of highest beauty and utmost impenetrableness, he says, then go to it with a vengeance. But if you merely obfuscate your work in order to hide from self-judgement within a dense thicket, then your Heart will drag you backwards through a hedge.

THE LENSGRINDER

n the arched gateway, a glass figure sits peacefully beneath a glass tree, studiously grinding lenses. The glass wind fails to stir its glass forelock. Glass dust seethes and settles around it, as it takes a glass breath into its glass lungs, tinkling like a chandelier.

Composed largely of lenses, the Lensgrinder studies everything but is blind to itself. It has two monocles attached to its glass waistcoat, one to observe the noumenon, and the other the phenomenon, but it can never remember which is which. Sometimes it wears them both together, but that rather cancels the effect. It grinds lenses to see far, lenses to see near, and lenses to see far too close for comfort.

The Lensgrinder is so focused on perfecting the apparatus of its observation that it has lost sight of what it is searching for.

As a concierge, it is less than ideal.

THE SILHOUÊTRES

Delving deeper into the shimmering halls, the visitor may witness flickering shapes slide out of view, and dancing figures streak fleetingly along the walls.
The Silhouêtres! In terror of their own work being judged inferior, they spent their lives imitating others', and now are merely a shadow of their former selves.

THE METICULANTS

 etween the skeletal columns, a shining figure moves with an oddly twisting motion. Metal glints in the gloom, and out struts the Encompass, its pointed legs held apart by a screw, its head a tiny ball of polished steel.

Montcorbier may try waltzing with it, and you may try too!

An Abacus sits at the base of a column, playing with itself. It fingers the beads of its chest gently as though telling the rosary. Beside it, the Method, lashed together from a collection of corsets, grimly tightens its own laces with its hooked teeth.

THE FOLLYGREE

The Follygree, glinting in the half-light, spins itself a nest of silver lace which sprouts out around it like a fern. Each frond curls into a spiral which holds another smaller spiral, and so on, and so on, until the last visible spiral spirals into nothingness. The Follygree itself has vanished under the branches.

The Follygree enjoyed embroidering its work until the meaning disappeared. It draped its art in gauze so it could not see its shape, lest that shape not be up to snuff.

But its vain Heart sought to recognise itself, and took offence at being denied its own image.

THE PIÑYADDAYADDA

oitering in an archway, gowned Masteralls take grave swings at a twirling, crepe-wrapped figure, beating at it with rolled up testimonials of their perfect right to do so.

The Piñyaddayadda had a sweet wisdom tooth and filled itself with trivia and miscellany so it had no appetite for anything substantial, namely its Vision. One whack on its cardboard carcass, and facts cascade everywhere.

The Masteralls, as a rule, prefer to beat one of their own, but otherwise roam the corridors, looking for flimsy arguments and things to critique.

One took a swing at Montcorbier the last time he passed through, although possibly that was a mistake.

It is happening a lot lately. Little errors. Carnations not quite where they should be. Odd looks.

But never mind.

THE POLYGLUTTON

mmense and babbling, a tongue-plant in a pot gibbers to itself on the side of the corridor. When approached, the babbling increases in volume, rising to a desperate cacophony.

The venerable Polyglutton sought to avoid the scrutiny of readers, so did nothing but scribble its poems in dead languages (which only about three people could understand) and private ciphers (which no-one could).

Montcorbier applauds and admires the academic artistry of its endeavours, as he's a collector of dialects and words himself, but admits there's little use in having the tongues of the four quarters at one's command if they fall on deaf ears (if you'll pardon the faintly confusing imagery, he says. Or don't pardon. That's rather the point of this place).

If the Polyglutton were wallowing in linguistics for art, or scholarship, or proverbial kicks, its Heart would have no quarrel with it. But the Heart knows when it's being lied to, whatever the vocabulary.

THE SOLIPSPHERE

 dull clink of stone echoes down the corridor, and a gigantic orb of olive jade rolls into view. Its inner spheres shimmy and jostle within an outer shell carved with graceful lotus flowers.

It is the Solipsphere, a hermetic artist, dwelling as perfect, internally consistent layers of immaculate self-reference, with no relation to the outside world.

As the sombre behemoth trundles past, through the briefly aligned holes of the nested carvings you may catch sight of a jagged edge, as one of the balls within ball has become a collection of shards (within balls within ball).

The Guide may have tried to bowl it down the corridor at one point. It's less sturdy than it looks.

The Solipsphere rolls sullenly onward, sounding like an ambulant bag of broken crockery.

THE DUALIST

ontinuing down the narrowing corridor, twinned figures will leap into your path, swords flashing. Behold, a Dualist, fighting its clone! (Which one was the original was a frequent duelling matter, although in truth they spawned via a sort of mitosis.)

The body of one is water; the other, flame. As they fight, the water clone evaporates into furious steam, re-forms and rains down upon the fire clone, which splutters and hisses as it is doused, but flares alive again seconds later.

The Dualist seems on the brink of merging with itself. Its two faces begin morphing together, then sharpen back into separateness. They glare at each other, and spring apart.

The Dualist spent all its time arguing with itself, trying to come up with both thesis and antithesis, argument and counter-argument.

It was so engaged in battle with its own thoughts it had no time for anyone else's.

THE EQUIPOISE

egal and dignified, an antiquated diplomatic artist trussed in a rope made of its own reasonableness and spinning a plate on its nose, hops across the corridor on one leg.

The Equipoise spent seventeen years on a theory proving people were inherently good.

This so displeased everyone, and they were so rude about it, that the poor soul spent another seventeen proving people were inherently knaves and asses.

In this the Equipoise was so utterly correct that the village burned down its house in admiration.

THE GNOMONICS

Winding tighter into the core of the spiral, the visitor will notice doors begin appearing in the iridescent ivory, swimming to the surface like sea-creatures breaching.

The first door is made of signposts cobbled together. Behind it, Gnomonics stalk musingly around on their wrought iron legs. Human sundials, their blind circular faces and triangular, pointed noses are turned endlessly upwards, seeking illumination.

But it is, alas, dark. And indoors.

The Gnomonics conjured philosophical quandaries that would never exist, and asked questions nobody wanted answered, to avoid dealing with what *did* exist and *was* in need of answering.

Do not even touch the door, or you will be trapped for days involved in a discussion about the absence of purple.

THE SUNMILER

archment forms the second door. A brass being with a glass sphere head sits at a desk, lit by a gas lamp. Before it a map bristles with mountains.

The figure traces the topography carefully with a quill of light. The artist's calliper legs scrape gently on the floor as it stretches them out before it. To its side lies a long scroll of numbers and arcane diagrams.

The Sunmiler counts sun-miles.

What are sun-miles you ask?

Land the sun touches.

Mountainous landscapes have more sun-miles than deserts, apparently. It has to do with surface area.

Is there any need for such observations?

Of course not.

THE VANITY PROJECTION

he third door is a single mirror. An infinity of yourselves greet you once behind it. Reflected endlessly in the hexagonal walls, a line of identical figures curving out into inconsequentiality.

There's an artist in here somewhere. But it's made of mirrors, so you must feel out with your foot before stamping a bit and stepping forward, as though temporarily blinded. When your own reflection suddenly appears before your face, the Vanity Projection is here!

Careful not to smudge it. It gets very irate!

You must then polish the Vanity Projection.

It is relieving to close the door and be singular again.

One can have too much of oneself.

THE MUTUAL ADMIRATION SOCIETY

 brass plaque on the next door proclaims:
The Mutual Admiration Society. Inside, two identical shining automatons bow relentlessly at each other. Hooked together, they move like synchronised metronomes, their copper gears squeaking and creaking rhythmically.

This is artistic self-obsession taken to the unusual level of actually involving another artist. Provided that artist is identical to yourself.

THE LEPIDOPTERROR

normous moths inside a glass conservatory buffet the air, creating a gusty turbulence that sweeps you off your feet as you try to enter the fifth room.

Amongst them, a white-cloaked Lepidopterror reeking of formaldehyde leaps frantically, endeavouring to impale the immortal insects with a specimen pin as large as a sword.

The Lepidopterror sought to nail down the meaning of existence through artistic experiments of questionable morality.

Ignoring that meaning may be ephemeral, changeable, and gone in a flash, and it is better, therefore, to observe and marvel than dissect.

Eventually its Heart pinned it to the Eternal Carnation.

THE HYBRIDISERS

ractising in the room across the way—the unfeasibly large room, considering it's towards the centre of the spiral—the Hybridisers design animals of types unconducive to sanity.

A sudden screech pierces the air as the Thorny Frogmouth becomes entangled with the Batalope. In answer, the Peawolf unfurls its magnificent plumage and howls. The Antaroo bounds joyfully, its feelers awhirl. A Giraffagon rubs its scaly wings on the vaulted ceiling, its long neck curling.

Montcorbier is very fond of the Giraffagon, and brings it flowers from the garden whenever he can.

THE GARLANDED & THE GOLDEN LION

own the corridor drifts a mist of gold, curdling in the dappled light. Luminous tendrils crawl up the pearlescent walls, and wander caressingly around a doorframe.

They sink to the floor, and snake across to coil around you, plucking at your coat-tails, or evening gown, or pantaloons, or whatever quotidian fiasco you are wearing at the time of your Heart-imposed visitation.

Behind the door is a dismal affair.

Roaring, a gold lion statue is lashed to a sacrificial altar. Various philosophers, crowned in floral halos, glowing like gas lamps in the haze, solemnly slice pieces off it with blades of light.

The Garlanded are endeavouring to see how much of the Golden Lion they can remove before it ceases to be a Golden Lion. What precise quantity of Golden Lion must you have, to know what you have is, in fact, a Golden Lion?

The Golden Lion objects to this quandary.

It is all very well to seek the essence of a thing, but what if that thing needs to retain the mystery of its essence and dies without it?

The rapidly diminishing beast paws mournfully at its bindings.

Sometimes, it becomes too much for Montcorbier, and he uses his ludicrous sword for something other than poking the fire in the tavern or pointing at things, and he strides forth and swings it through the lion's hovering tormentors.

The Garlanded then disperse, unharmed, and regroup in the corners of the room, where they hang, waiting.

Montcorbier, meanwhile, shakes his épée, to which wisps of sophistry still cling, and returns to his state of apathy.

It is not his fault the Golden Lion got into this predicament.

Or perhaps it is.

Yes, it is.

But he doesn't know how to stop it.

He doesn't know what to do.

THE METROYSHKA

n the streaks of sunlight by the courtyard at the centre of the nautilus, a glossy, rotund figure made of wood is painting a larger replica of itself.

It touches up the final eyelash, decides it is satisfied with its own depiction, cracks the replica open, and leaps into the hollowness, which shuts behind it like a clam. A new Metroyshka shell spawns immediately. The now-enlarged doll begins to paint the even larger version.If you watch a while, the process repeats itself.

What is its crime, decided by its Heart?

It is engorged with selfhood.

Instead of all roads leading to Rome, the Metroyshka had decided, in life, that all roads should lead to Metroyshka. It painted only self-portraits, wrote only semi-transparently autobiographical novels, sung only of its own grievances. So absorbed was it with its own depiction that eventually it could produce nothing else. And thus, if you lose interest in the world, your work will cease to interest *it*.

The light sheen of varnish over the doll's latest face is blistering under the sun.

THE OULIPOUBEROUS

truggling to swallow its own tail, a colossal snake, vermilion eyes rolling, thrashes pointlessly in the courtyard. Its violent effort crushes it up against the opalescent pillars, such that it bulges a little in between them like an overstuffed sausage.

Its motley-hued skin changes from violet to magenta, sap green to scarlet, azurite to mauve, and so on through the wild spectrum, except for the more unsavoury patches where the serpent has been lying too long on the damp ground.

A flamboyant, self-consuming, self-defeating creature writhing futilely in a trap of its own devising is certainly something Montcorbier can sympathise with.

One day, he hopes, the previously mentioned Metroyshka will grow so vast it topples over on account of the weight of its gigantic, bloated head and crush the city. Which would be a mercy for all involved.

THE COY

rapped inside the circle of snake is a pond that tries to vanish when anyone looks at it. It contains Coy: large splendid fish who avoid each other's gaze. However, as each of their scales is a mirror which reflects every other Coy in the pond, creating an Indra's Net of Coy in every direction, this reticence is obviously a sham.

THE IBID & RARIFIED

recariously around the perimeter of the Coy Pond stalks the ibis-like Ibid, tall, gangly, and mournful. Every so often, it elongates its lustrous beige neck and warbles a plaintive:

'Ibid! Ibid! Iiiiiii-bid!'

A small, robed Soliplost—the Rarified—strides high above on ivory stilts, garbling down:

'B^lathna_u g_i.bblywomba bezenkemb_i.t T_i^t t_i^t! P^oth_ily crample_i!'

It has, alas, forgotten how to speak to lesser mortals.

THE RROSE

lourishing and fecund, a beautiful garden blooms beyond the pond. Trees grafted with manifold-specied branches hold fruits which ripen by the hour. Sweating purple figs split their skin, dusky apples swell, and pomegranates grow shiny and bulbous.

Unfortunately, as they can only ever be picked between 3.03 a.m. and 3.17 a.m. every second Tuesday, and nobody knows what day it is, and it is always noon, the fruits hang in a perpetual state of uncertainty, somewhere between ripe and rot.

A gardener with a face like a rose is tending a rose garden planted in the shape of a rose. The roses' faces follow the gardener like the sun, as the Rrose moves deep into the bud, a loving, prying worm.

THE TORTICULTURIST &
HAUGHTYCULTURIST

all and gnarled, a twisted creature with limbs all knotted and whorled is busy contorting trees into immaculate shapes, as in life it crafted neologisms that nobody understood. Slowly, stubbornly, the Torticulturist bends a mighty branch to its will, straining the tree against its nature so intensely it causes beads of milky sap to burst from its own brow. Soon an ear-rattling crack shakes the peaceful gardens, and shards of wood ricochet off in all directions.

From a hedge, exotic flowers curl upwards towards the sun. The Haughtyculturist, once a fierce protector of the dictionary, and nemesis of the Torticulturist, frenziedly cuts them off. More appear, coiling relentlessly towards the light. More shearing, more chopping. The dead new words lie all around, blackened.

Nearby, elements are being trained against their natures. Fire is made geometric, stone forced to liquefy, and the wind winds around wicker framework like a trained poodle.

The Reverse Alchemist, overlooking this unnatural affair, sits on a tripod slowly turning gold to lead.

A glorious blossoming tree erupts at the centre of the garden. A sign pinned to the tree passionately implores the Monkey King not to steal its peaches, but every day Montcorbier tears it down.

He would welcome a visit.

And now we come, alas, to arguably the worst place in the city. If you have tolerated Montcorbier long enough to follow him here, you may perhaps wish you'd stayed in the tavern.

We shan't linger.

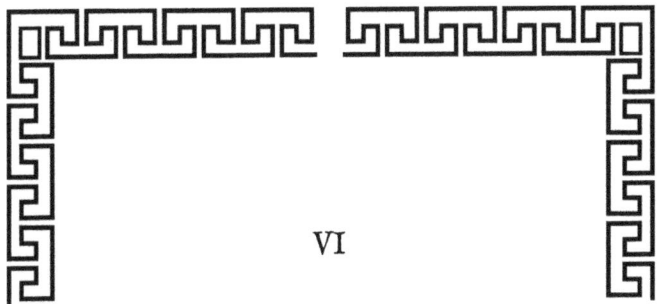

VI

THE COLONAUSEAM

DESECRATION OF ART

PILLAGERS

BLEACHED BY THE PITILESS SUN, THE TRAVERTINE STEPS OF THE COLOSSAL AMPHITHEATRE LIE WORN BY THE PASSAGE OF COUNTLESS FEET.

A black bird slices across the noxious blue sky, its cry twisted and sour, echoing off the limestone blocks along with the sullen beat of a goat-skin drum.

In the arena, blood branches and dries in charnel dendrites on rusted blades, or sinks away into the sands. The heat shimmers, baking the stench of offal rising from the ring into something cryptic and antique.

In the scorched dust, a mother-of-pearl rhinoceros, gleaming in the haze, fights a flame-tipped falcon, tall as a horse. Both human-faced, they are deranged with fever, prodded into a fatal fury by the long lances of the cricket-like jesters who hop around them.

Vultures wing down to stab at the heaped carcasses, the remnants of a thousand tournaments, and howls and unhappy screeches poison the air.

Naked, hysterical gore worshippers, sanguine-painted, pull each other around the activities in a chilling circle dance.

Fallen knights lie crinkled like macabre decorations on the boundaries, glinting dully in the sun.

THE MATTER D'OR

t the centre of the raucous crowd, a gruesome spectacle unfurls. To thwart the Goryators, the Matter d'Or, a mighty bay minotaur, has gored itself on its own sword.

It shudders and falls forward upon one knee, and with weary grace sweeps off its hat, and bows to the roaring audience, sweat dripping from its brow into a subsiding pool of blood. The Matter d'Or is dying from the injury that pride has inflicted and pride would not allow to heal. It presses its hat against the wound and bows once more.

A little brass band plays the Pasodoble.

THE GORYATORS

eaving terror in their wake, the Goryators are built of slabs of meat, some marbled, others raw and sinewy, but all are cruel, squalid, and bestial.

They reek of pestilence and the taint of their office: the obliteration of ideals. Truth, Freedom, Justice: all the usual suspects lie broken at their feet. They then throw the symbolic body to the crowd, a company of toga-clad jackals which, delirious, tear it apart.

THE DESECREATOR

verlooking the whole atrocious affair is a shining satyr, its blond curls glistening in the light. Its bone-white toga leaches oils and perfumes into the heavy air.

The Desecreator is in charge of the Colonauseam's 'entertainment'.

It is bored. It is wilful. It does not care for beauty.

Sometimes, in life, it had made intricate, entrancing things, but only by accident, and it broke them swiftly.

Occasionally, the populace had fallen in love with one of these transient, accidental objects. And then the Desecreator had been merciless. It reached its full potential for horror.

For it did not understand why its creation was adored, only that it had gained attention. It therefore sought, like the opportunist it was, to maximise this interest, regardless of the cost to the creation itself.

Many a great idea, widely or fervently loved, had been ruined through the Desecreator's greed or carelessness.

THE HYPOGEUM

arkness and dappled light commingle in the hypogeum, a hollowed-out maze of termite-tunnels and chambers under the Colonauseam, where the abhorrent troglodytes of the city lurk, glutting its alcoves. Those who profited from the perversion of art, or fed upon its brutalised form, have contrived a thriving market around the detritus scavenged from every corner of this chaotic, unfinished land.

Leftover fragments of useless ornaments, lost things, and broken armour from unwinnable skirmishes. Curiosities washed ashore from the Inkspill Sea. Like visitors. Or indeed, like yourself, one day, perhaps.

Grime, unmolested for an age, clogs the crumbling stone arcades, and a throng of Pilferers and Peddlers weave around the haggard columns.

The Pilferers cloak their rodent-like, fidgety bodies in meticulously stitched patchwork, whilst the Peddlers, five feet tall, resemble large, shiny cockroaches in floor-length black leather coats.

Both species move with startling speed upon their hind legs.

The Pilferers scurry back and forth, bringing Purposes dredged from the moat, to be hefted onto blackened platforms, sliced and mangled, their silvery, iridescent scales scraped from their flanks and into wicker baskets to be dried. Bottled Scents of Purpose are sold to dilettantes, who promptly lose them.

The Unreliable Narrator keeps artistic devices for sale inside a bulging valise:

Lampshades, gaslights, mortar for fourth walls, MacGuffins, red herrings, foreshadows ...

Noise and filth entwine in all directions, and a light sheen of grease covers every surface. A stench of decay hangs in the thick, viscous air.

A haze of humanoid effluvia floats by, arm in arm with the Decoupage, which envelops itself in stolen histories, cut up and heavily glossed over.

THE TITILLATORS

hastly Titillators sell tickets to even ghastlier unseen shows. Their oily, swollen bodies are prickly with clumped hairs and doused in sickly colognes. They buzz like engorged bluebottle flies. Their lurid dust wrapper jackets are tainted, foxed and seedy. Cheap touts, they chirp before the jostling crowd, trash sticking to them.

THE MISERY MAKARS

n the alcoves, a cluster of more sinister beings stands silent. Draped in tooth necklaces and shawls of shrunken skins, the Misery Makars peddle their graveyard wares under the archways where a cold wind blows, where elsewhere there is no wind.

You may try to see their faces beneath their hooded cloaks, but perhaps it's better if you don't.

Mummified husks lean against the stone walls in leathery, horrific rictus, price-tagged and dis-embandaged, ready to grind up and apply to whatever work the buyer chooses.

The Misery Makars are the Carnations who considered historical abomination and horror their Muse. Where there is misery, there is always a Makar.

Was there an era from which the spirit recoiled in anguish? A murdering of millions of souls? A reign that threw its heart into a dungeon? A Misery Makar wrote a popular, sentimental book about it.

Not to illuminate, nor educate, nor to bear witness, nor to protest, nor to cope with private sorrow, but simply to draw the public's tearful gaze upon their own countenance, and to expand their wallet in the process.

With their talents, they might have created anything under the sun, but this tragedy already had an audience, so why not capitalise on its grief?

Humanity has a morbid fascination with acts of inhumanity, and from it, the Misery Makar made their coin.

So this atrocity became a fashionable stage play, or a series of deeply tasteful pastel portraits of the corpses.

In only the best galleries, naturally.

THE VULTURES

Swaggering around the wretched scene are the enterprising Vultures, each small and gristly, bloodied knuckle of a head poking out from a feather boa.

If disaster struck, they were there to make the most of it. If a city was under siege and the populace turned to eating rats, leather boots, and each other, the Vultures were waiting to write a song about it.

Not for the benefit of the besieged, obviously—they have no time left in their unfathomable schedule—but for the voyeurs farther afield, those sensitive souls outside, and very far away, who wish to suffer vicariously, and purely for catharsis.

THE UNDERSEER

Towering on stilt-like legs, the cadaverous Underseer, the master Misery Makar, stalks through the malignant, scrofulous hordes. Gaunt and rotting, its powder-caked face leers down, slick lipstick a-gleam on its bared teeth.

Wending its haunting, predatory way through the redolent crowd, its moth-eaten cloak, edged with dyed fur, drags in the refuse by its feet. It keeps a keen and bloodshot eye upon Montcorbier.

On the splintered platform, stained with pigment, tattered individuals stand bowed and broken, canvas bodies frayed or slashed down the middle. Crumpled fictional forms hunch upon the steps, their torsos bleeding ink. Some have been fleshed out as characters, which makes it even worse.

The Underseer oversees this sideshow of sorts, of abandoned beings from neglected novels, half-finished heroes from half-finished stories, tentative pentimenti lost behind the subsequent layers. All found their way to the Eternal Carnation, for a little of the artist's soul has passed into them. When the artists fell, they dragged with them their incomplete creations. Once in the city, their creators knew them no longer, being occupied in the everlasting dance they had choreographed for themselves. Unclaimed, the innocents were rounded up by the Underseer and sent to the Colonauseam, there to ply whatever useful traits their progenitors had afforded them before death. Some could sing; others, fight. A few unfortunates, burdened with the private memories of their authors, had detailed capabilities, but most were useless. So the Misery Makars made use of them.

They broke characters of all description into new shapes, cobbled and stitched them together to make them saleable. Others, irrespective of skill, were put to the ring, there to battle hybrids built thoughtlessly by the Hybridisers in the Temple of Fo-Elpmet-Eht, who had been consumed only with noble thoughts of invention.

Once, a bound creature, half magpie, half highwayman, being led down towards the scaffold, passed by the Guide and studied him intently.

But the Guide said nothing. Did nothing. Looked away, as the Makars hoisted the creature upon a gallows where it spun awkwardly, cawed thrice, and then had its wings broken.

It was an eternal pity.

But why did Montcorbier look away?

Because he is a coward.

There is no other explanation.

Although, perhaps guilt would also suffice.

THE PALIMPSEST

High noon—as ever, as always—back in the glare of the arena, the sun boils the crucible of a crowd grown even more boisterous and bloodthirsty. Goryators drag the Golden Lion, stolen roaring from the Temple, over the foul sands towards the Vultures. The crowd falls silent, and across the arena, swimming in the blackness of an alcove, a wraithlike creature appears.

Tall, spindly, and white, this spectre of paper and parchment floats out into the air, a skeletal butterfly. Pauses, quivering. Surges down to slice across the sands, its tattering veil rustling in the windless air. It would seem a mirage with all its ripples and oscillations, but the turmoil in the dust and the whispering of friction betrays its reality.

It is the Palimpsest.

An executioner, sent to kill off characters, for shock, for catharsis, anything to draw a crowd. It destroys a favoured creation to bring a tear, or just because it can.

No-one likes the Palimpsest.

It plays with your heart.

The strangest thing occurred one day.

The Palimpsest is usually under the control of the Vandal, but this time its ringside box was empty. Of late, the box has often been empty.

But yes, on this particular day, the Palimpsest made an odd pirouette, and glided towards Montcorbier, scythe raised, blinding in the sun.

Then it stopped.

One might say, a terrible shame it did.

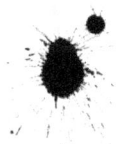

The dreadful thing about this city, aside from the obvious, is the equity of its entry requirements.

It may draw no artistic distinction between an allegory on a chapel ceiling and a painted kitten on a piece of crockery—a good thing! Because how can anyone judge the Vision of the Heart?—but it also sees no difference between a kind or rotten soul.

One might be a murderer, a truly vile scoundrel, but if your Heart has no quarrel with your Vision, indeed, your Vision itself may be monstrous, then you will not end here. Likewise, the gentlest being, empathetic and wise, if they fail in their Vision's depiction, and their Heart is a tyrannous bastard, it will drag them to this city and keep them here forever.

It is not fair, nor honourable in any way. But that is the nature of this place. It is built upon a private philosophy, which knows only its own logic.

Wrest yourself from its ridiculous, sophistic bonds if you can. Montcorbier has tried.

He is still trying.

Montcorbier has some scruples, he says. At least three. Possibly four. In a furnishing vein, for example, he doesn't think a bull's head should be made into a hat-rack, an elephant's foot into an umbrella stand, an Attic urn turned into a piss-pot in the local tavern, and more generally, he believes artists shouldn't use their talents to lend strength to horrors upon the earth.

Beyond that, he cares very little.

But by Alighieri, let us not preach.

This city might well have been designed by a Misery Makar. Who else could so damn their fellow artists? What manner of soulless, heartless villain, revenging themselves upon the world for their own inadequacies?

But perhaps they've learned their lesson?

Perhaps having crafted it, they regret it bitterly?

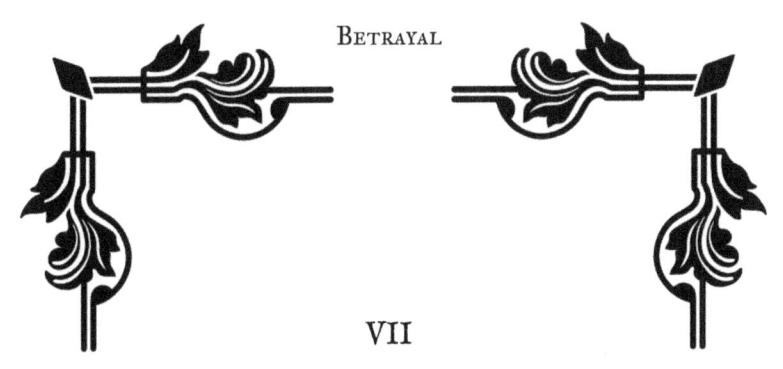

VII

THE PARADE

BETRAYAL OF ART

Punchinellos

WINDING UP THE MOUNTAIN STREETS, THE VISITOR WILL FIND THE SOUND OF DRUMS AND SHRIEKS FROM THE COLONAUSEAM FADE MERCIFULLY INTO SILENCE.

At the summit, the city flattens out into a long checker-board street lined with flags bearing nonsensical crests and symbols. Twisted, wrought iron guards stand sombrely against the flanking stone walls, the flames of their torches almost swallowed by the eternal noonday glare. And here we find the sole type of Punchinello:

THE MÂCHINATIONS

igantic puppets spin silently on parade, knocking and scratching their ballooned, papier-mâché heads against one another, staggering and wheeling, painted, dead-eyed faces gleaming in the ceaseless sun.

Gods, monarchs, politicians, and saints, speeding up and slowing down, buoyed by their own procession, following some private, churning rhythm, eerie and syncopated. The unstable waltz of something wounded, still dragging itself around.

Some fight, head-butting like mountain goats. Others jerk on frenzied strings, pulled and yanked, hither and thither, all under the merciless burning light. In a hysterical, unstoppable dance, they whirl. Doomed to dance until they die (were they not already dead). Destined to parade eternally as a hollow mockery of the idols they served in life.

For the Mâchinations, through cowardice or greed, sold their talents to tyrannous regimes and hate-riddled causes, dressed themselves up in cruelty, and draped bloodshed around their necks like an evening scarf.

The court artist who, for a living, paints a pleasing portrait of an eccentric but benign king is a different animal from these artists who painted pleasing portraits of monstrosities, flattering to those who committed them.

The Mâchinations used their skills to further the reach of despots and peddled inflammatory creeds in which they did not believe. They trampled over the bodies of their fellows, their tread made heavier by the weight of the gold gained by their betrayal.

Did their friend write a play that was not quite *sound*? Did it threaten the integrity of their mighty homeland? Was their neighbour a danger to themselves? No matter! The Mâchination would see they found a new home. Forever.

But listen!

Something different in the silent parade. Rupturing the noiselessness.

An odd beat flickers through the tumultuous crowd, a crickety clicking. Castanets suddenly clatter to the forefront, and a violin slices through the scorching air. A thin, metallic, embittered sound, like the frustrated slash of a sabre.

The note climbs, arrives, eddies at its height. An extended moment of exaltation! Illumination! Held endlessly. Torturously, the violin constantly peaks, the moment breaking, over and over, the dancers in torment. Nerves flayed. The crowd tense as rigging.

A line of empty-headed puppets emerge from the assembly like errant crabs, pincering in emerald and russet silk, trailing string. Taut thighs mincing in a nutcracker manoeuvre. Swollen paper heads whispering as they brush together.

A sudden movement!

Montcorbier has leapt between the dancers! His sulky face pursed in concentration, his Turkish slippers stirring the pigmented powder shed from the painted heads into tufts of riotous, coloured clouds.

He is a terrible dancer, but never mind.

The castanets return, and Montcorbier springs as though stung into the empty circle, drawing his arms up. A praying mantis! A being possessed, his eyes glazed and despairing, he performs a parody of a Bulerias. He dances viciously, furiously. Very badly. Grabs a puppet and morphs his ad hoc flamenco into a maddened Mazurka, spinning his goggle-eyed partner wildly out of line as the violins wail at speed.

Blank-faced mannequins wearing all manner of masks pass by, and one—tall and imperious—hooks Montcorbier by the arm. It presses its sleek snouted head towards him. He shudders and draws back. The creature follows, clasps its rotten hand around his throat. The mask slips, revealing the leering, cadaverous face of the Underseer, crept up from the Colonauseam!

But see!

This time Montcorbier strikes at it!

It groans and reels, turns molten black, and splashes across the cobblestones. Above, a bruise spreads sullenly over the sky, blocking out the sun and darkening the parade. The blot becomes mottled and malignant, then shimmers into nothingness.

The sun reappears.

A great nodule of ornamental plaster breaks away from a balcony and falls with a clunk to the paving stones. Montcorbier jumps like a startled cat, flattening himself against the wall.

'Sapristi!' he cries.

A cluster of vacant saints spins past, whirling away down the street, shrinking into miniatures. The dancers shuffle the cloud of dust into the depths of the parade.

Silence resumes.

But perhaps Montcorbier's music will last this time?

Perhaps the city will forgive him?

Perhaps they will forget?

Because Montcorbier remembers. He remembers fandangos. Accordions in alleyways. In tiny courtyards, castanets under the orange trees. He would bring the memories of his travels to this hell, but the Architect is against him.

There is no music in the City of Lost Intentions

that is not distorted, broken, a plague on the ear. The betrayed Heart won't allow it.

Despite this, Montcorbier tries to teach the Carnations to dance. To the music he can hear! He fails!

Ah! But he will keep trying!

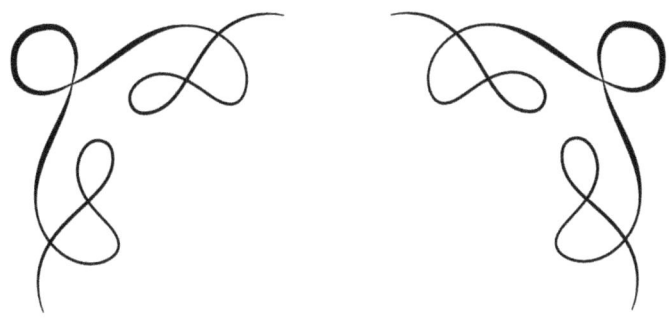

THE BOOKMARK

A SMALL, WHITEWASHED FOLLY OCCUPIES THE HIGHEST POINT OF THE MOUNTAIN CITY.

Old and crumbling, it is bare of ornament, save for a slight Corinthian curl to its columns.

Moss creeps up from the foundations over the worn lime. Everything is silent and still.

Inside a room walled like a columbarium with boxes of typefaces and ink bottles, a nest of crumpled paper holds the Bookmark, cradled as gently as an egg.

Its glistening sphere of a head flickers with images

of all the artistic fears and foibles under the sun.

The Bookmark can remember committing no crime in life, indeed can remember nothing at all except paperwork. It has come fully fledged into existence as a quill-pusher.

In truth, it was born of a Camembert and port dream, but it doesn't need to know that.

The rich mahogany leather of its torso lightens into expansive wings of illuminated parchment, now crumpled behind the back of its chair. A magnificent array of book-tassels dangle down like stoles.

Two weevils roam its desk within an imprisoning brass-bound magnifying glass. They writhe happily in Montcorbier's presence.

If the Bookmark's face could smile, it wouldn't have. You are not meant to come to it during office hours.

But all its hours are office hours.

When Montcorbier ignores this, and visits anyway, the wings of the Bookmark unfurl with a sound like dry leaves, and its aura of bureaucratic weariness increases tenfold.

The Bookmark is a gentle soul whose function is to record all those who fall into the city, even those who merely wander too close to its peripheries (albeit writ in a separate ledger).

It catalogues them by Misdeed.

It has a lot of work to do.

For the Architect left a blueprint of the city. A scribbled draft, some poor sketches, above all, a commentary, running page upon page, of ruminations upon ruination, pasquinades on the predicaments of artists, crude caricatures of artistic crises, garnered from a decade of bizarre investigation.

The Bookmark inherited this fiasco, and endeavours to make sense of it. It has absorbed the philosophy, so called, behind the Architect's intentions, and files the new arrivals to the city accordingly, although in its own idiosyncratic style (it has an unquenchable, unfortunate thirst for ornamental lettering).

But of late, something plagues the Bookmark, and it merely scrawls illegibly, its mind far afield.

For Montcorbier has begun to steal these pages and rework them to his own liking. He is, in fact, writing a guidebook to the city.

At first he disagreed with the Architect's commentary, so scratched it out, bit by bit, day by day. Now, it seems, he disagrees with the idea behind the city itself!

Which is absurd.

Does a lock disagree with a cage?

Does it fight against the thing which is its own nature?

Why, of course it does. Particularly if it is a saboteur at heart. But a lock both protects and imprisons, so which is Montcorbier?

Is he the sword that both slays and saves?

He does not know anymore.

He has a part to play, and it is sometimes, irritatingly said, that there is freedom in duty. So why does he complain? He who has the run of the city, he who largely does as he pleases?

Because it is the freedom of a goat upon a tether, cavorting in a circle.

A happiness measured by thimblefuls.

Sometimes, he thinks how he might throw a spanner in the tiresome works of this whole farrago.

What, for example, if the Carnations knew that the Architect of this hell, the object of their hatred, and the city's deepest foe, was closer than they thought? What if he told them that? What if he told them who it was?

Would that not be a dreadful thing? For them to know the monster at the heart of the labyrinth and call it kin? Would that not be disquieting? What if they knew them intimately?

Fortunately, Montcorbier says, he tries not to know anyone intimately.

But perhaps the Carnations know already? Indeed, they almost certainly know.

That is beginning to become clear.

Perhaps, in turn, the Architect has grown tired of his creations? Perhaps he has begun to despise them. Perhaps because they have begun to despise *him*.

And why should they not?

He has caged them, and he is the cage himself. Yet he has no power here. He has no hope of escape. This place is one monumental prison, and he is locked in.

And he hates the sun. He burns easily.

The city should have been set at night. Cities are beautiful in the dark. Only lanterns, tavern lights, and stars to see by. The underside of the tapestry.

He'd have made the stars come out.

But now he cannot.

His Heart won't allow it.

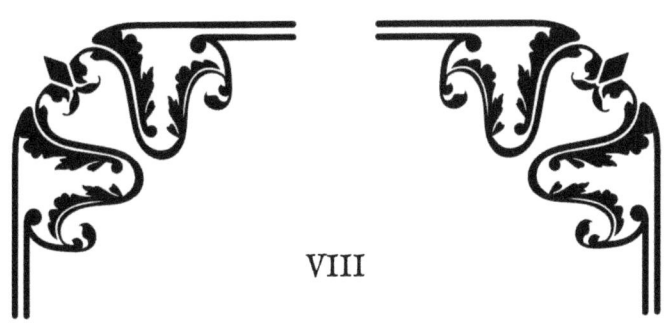

VIII

THE UNDERMINE

SABOTAGE OF ART

PYRRHICS

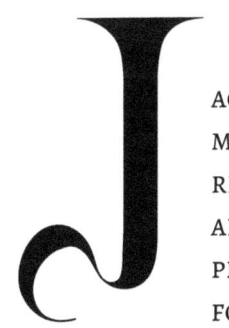AGGED AND SOLITARY, THE MOUNTAIN THE CITY CLINGS TO IS RIDDLED WITH ECHOING CAVERNS AND WINDING TUNNELS, A RATHER PERILOUS STATE OF AFFAIRS FOR A FOUNDATION.

The Underminers wrought this fine but dangerous work, those in whom life's lack of intrinsic purpose and the absence of absolutes induced such despair that they hobbled themselves mid-quest, thus saving themselves the effort of marching to no end.

Also, there is a terrible appeal to ruining everything.

When life is meaningless, why not fall upon your sword? Fly towards the sun with wax wings? At least it proves your autonomy.

One enters this subterranean maze via the back of the Bookmark's folly, where a simple green curtain conceals the ominous mouth of the Undermine.

A gloomy cave, sepulchral and musty, fanged with ancient stalactites and draped in dusty shawls of calcium carbonate greets the visitor once inside. Limestone walls parch the air, tightening the skin. Snaking down into the mountain, rails running along its floor, a tunnel.

A mass will detach itself from the shadows, glide down the track, and halt. This small train carriage—which looks suspiciously like a halved whisky barrel on wheels—will be your transportation.

Montcorbier will sombrely fold his long limbs into the barrel, and shift his coat to make room for his reluctant companion. He smells of soot and stale wine, and a hint of fermented clove from the decaying carnation on his lapel.

The barrel will judder back to life with a loud clank and shunt down the tunnel into darkness.

The walls are made of shimmering hematite, polished to high reflection by the endless traffic of artists passing through and down to their self-hewn hell.

190

THE UNDERMINERS

hough sight is impossible, the sound of activity is everywhere in the dull chink of iron upon rock. In the distance, an occasional spark leaps out into the void, briefly lighting the glistening walls.

As the tunnel widens into a grotto, Montcorbier will light the barrel lamp, bringing the whole scene into startling relief.

Hulking or frail, crystalline or cloudy, mineral figures stalk stiffly around the cave and cast flickering shades on the rock face as they hack deep into the mountain. Some resemble rough boulders, others seem a lace of glass. The Underminers' sharp multifaceted faces shine in the lamplight.

One stony forehead blossoms into a golden pyrite sun, the gleaming orb suspended in the grey shale of its brow. A stalactite creature drips to the floor, its ivory eyelids drooping.

Crimson crocoite bristles in spikes, rising from a bowed back into a petrified forest of blood. Rich purple grapes of botryoidal chalcedony bunch with the motion of muscles. Gelatinous, pomegranate-seed garnets erupt from white rhyolite and shift into eyes and mouths.

Agonised expressions are caught in clearest rock crystal, delicate phantoms etched in layers. Silvery mica skin shimmers like a mineraloid cicada wing.

A fluorite Underminer, translucent in bands of emerald and lilac, flares up when it passes before the lantern, glowing like a leadlight window in the darkness.

Tortured and twisted, lustrous and thorny, a creature made of native copper claws at itself, tearing away from its own ore.

Shot through with a comet trail of gold, a rutilated Underminer attacks a seam of quartz. Behind it, its tourmalinated companion, needled with black, drags the broken quarry away.

They all carry picks, raised dourly and doggedly against the very walls that had formed them. They undermine the city as in life they undermined themselves.

THE BLACKWICKS

Montcorbier will extinguish the lamp as the barrel trundles into the next cavern, far smaller than the last. Silence surrounds, even the barrel wheels muted to nothingness, as it rolls on into seeming absence.

In the blackness, the stifling exhalation of doused flames and snuffed candles fills the air—this is the form the incorporeal occupants of the cavern take.

For you are in the company of those who removed themselves from the mortal coil by philosophical choice, not tragic compulsion. The swiftest form of undermining. And the most certain.

Try not to inhale the smoke. It's only respectful.

Lantern relit, the barrel continues its downward journey.

THE FOREVERMORE

eathers litter the floor of the first of nine caves. Lice-ridden wings scrape and twitch as the Forevermore perches on a fraying footstool.

Framed pictures slump on the soot-clogged walls, each one a portrait of suffering. Moth-eaten tapestries flank the paintings, stretched in greasy webs over the blackened rock, lit by sickly gas lamps. A threadbare paisley rug lies tattered on the warped wood floor. The air is thick, and laced with carbon monoxide.

The Forevermore cannot breathe.

It is hallucinating, its feathers stiff with fear. Nightmares fill its once methodical mind.

And this was its intent.

The Forevermore addled itself with toxins, starved and suffocated its brain, as an aid to epiphany. Its hacking cough shakes the scratchy shawl draped over its thin form. It pulls more smoke in through its pipe, the tobacco stale and mouldy. A pot boils sullenly on the stovetop, in the water a single stone.

Monsters march about the Forevermore's hollow breast. It clutches them to its heart.

THE MOTHPYRE

ilvery dust coats the walls of the second cave, shining in the light of a six-foot flame into which an immense moth flings itself in perpetuity. The flutters of the ancient creature scatter more silver motes into the air.

It dances in a tantalisingly close circle around its scourge, then whirls towards it. Entering the fire, the Mothpyre blazes up, writhing, falls to ashes, then reforms and rises again to throw itself once more in desperation against the light.

The Mothpyre created a beacon of its torment and wrecked itself eternally upon its false shore.

THE LOCKSMITH

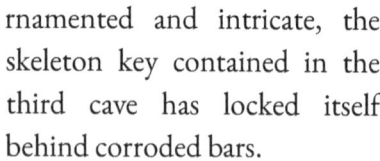rnamented and intricate, the skeleton key contained in the third cave has locked itself behind corroded bars.

The Locksmith tempted fate in the hope it would rid it of the demands of its Vision. It left lamps burning on its papers. Sculpted with cheap marble, with a flawed internal vein. Built on fault lines, or on the slopes of volcanos.

With its soul rusted over, peeling off in flakes of iron oxide, the Locksmith watches its manuscript smoulder on the stone floor outside its gate. In agony, it tries to reach its work! Yet it is locked in by its own design.

Groaning in ceaseless horror, it drags its crumbling visage across the worn bars of its prison, oblivious to its audience.

THE MIDNIGHT OILER

ighting the fourth cave, a wax figure courts another flame. The Midnight Oiler, in thrall to its muse. For every portion of itself it feeds to the fire, the flame returns an illumined glimpse of eternity, of its Vision.

For this, it is willing to sacrifice its health, its very substance. From its hands pour forth purest wax which hardens in garlands. It forces them into the self-sustained forge.

The fire flares, and briefly the artist sees its Vision before the embers claim it again.

The more of itself it gives to its muse, the less it has of itself to create its art. When one is a slave to one's inspiration, one has no time for anything else.

THE LOUCHE CANNON

hen anyone enters the long, fifth cave, a rumbling begins in the darkness, underscored by equine screams and the clattering of steel wheels on cobbles. Lanterns swing and dance in the distance and a carriage careens into view, drawn by four spittle-flecked, maddened horses, driven by the Louche Cannon, racing its Vision towards death. It hurtles by in a tumultuous riot of wind, upsetting the visitor's whisky barrel and sending its occupants tumbling into the dust.

THE MARTINGALE

B eneath a mammoth silver coin in the sixth cave, the Martingale trembles, bowed like Atlas, straining to keep its heavy burden aloft.

The enormous disc is pressing slowly and relentlessly down, always balanced on its edge between heads and tails.

The Martingale's shoulders shake. A single bullet shifts and clunks in the chamber of its chest, from death to life and back to death, whenever the gambler moves.

Black and red roulette eyes spin despairingly. If it could only put down the coin, it would leave the cave and resume its work.

It is hoping the coin will crush it first.

THE IMBIBER

lood-red wine pours from the mouth of the seventh cave, spilling out into the tunnel and welling over the tracks.

Inside, the Imbiber stands in a bottle filling with wine. The Imbiber's mouth is level with the burgundy tears. It drinks deeply, its eyes closed.

If the Imbiber does not drink, it drowns. It is doomed either way. But at least when it drinks, it can see. See what, you ask? The roof of its glass prison? No, a long vista. A thousand li. Or perhaps lees is more accurate. And upon that vista it sees its Vision.

When it does not drink, it is blind.

In the wine-flooded valleys of its mind, it feels a river flowing, uncoiling outwards to some unknown sea. It longs to touch the ships that sail upon those waters. It can fathom no greater pleasure than to seek the boundless, even if it must exile itself from life.

Once, it cast itself into the river, and was carried out beyond the shallows. Was hurled, illumined by its Vision, upon the barest rock, far at sea. It saw no other land. It had no boat. Its desire to remain upright upon that rock, gazing at its Vision, was stronger than its desire to return to shore.

Eventually the wine-dark sea knocked the Imbiber from its watchtower.

It washed up here. Forever.

Who can reassure the Imbiber its vigil was not in vain?

For this is the fourth fear mentioned in the Piazza.

One day, Reason rambles into your swank artistic affair, and pulls the rug from under your feet. All art is subjective! it cries. It has no true value under the sun! Suddenly your poetry, or pottery, or performance, is charmless, worthless, pointless.

Reason has shot your pole star from the sky. What will you do now you have lost your bearings?

There are three options, and one of them is lying, another Undermining, and the last is to devote yourself to the practice of the Subjective Absolute, but that is a matter mercifully outside the purview of this ostensible guidebook.

THE FRONTLINER

rom the eighth cave, immense heat boils forth, drenched with a sickly odour of rot and medicinal ointments, iodine, and burning, bitter herbs.

The inside resembles the ruins of a broken hut. Tattered canvas ranges over the walls, and a stench of malaise and death fill the chamber. A malarial yellow miasma cloaks the sparse furnishings. Maggots trail over the floor. A skeletal figure paces feverishly, wrapped in soiled bandages, sweating blood.

The Frontliner threw themselves into the path of conflict and suffering, and made themselves a sacrifice upon the altar of humanity.

They went to war because it was a death with corners. With outlines. They did not have to think too deeply about their Vision when they could walk in the dreadful shadow of another's—when they could replace the horrors of their own mind with the horrors of a multitude.

THE VILLAINELLE

Winding down the tunnel, the barrel will shudder to a stop outside the ninth and final cave. There is silence, save for the trickle of water.

A narrow, deep pit is bored into the middle of the cave floor. At the bottom of the pit is a *human*—of all things in this phantasmagorical city—snaggle-locked and filthy, bedecked in silk brocade.

They open their feverish, marsh-hued eyes, give a weak gesture of appeal with a long, pale hand, then drop it back upon their chest.

Whenever Montcorbier meets their gaze, an enormous tremor shakes the mountain. In the bowels of the Undermine, the lantern plunges into darkness. Groans and clangs resound through the tunnels as the foundations settle.

Of late, Montcorbier has been looking at the human often. But we shall say no more about this. Not at this time, anyway.

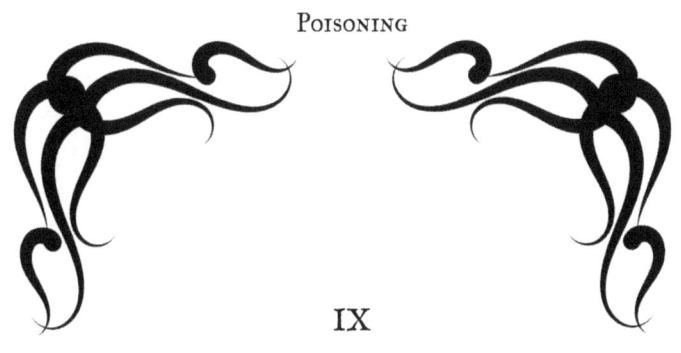

IX

THE CALDERA OF SCABS

POISONING OF ART

PICKSORES

BURIED DEEP BENEATH THE MOUNTAIN CITY IN A CAVERN AS FATHOMLESS AS THE HEAVENS, A VOLCANIC LANDSCAPE BUCKLES UNDER THE FORCE OF ITS INTERNAL TUMULT.

Miles of scabrous oxblood surface stretch out, hardened and ancient. In the centre, a tremendous crater gapes, a wound within the earth, fissured with crimson gashes. Virulent and lava-like, a substance brews venomously beneath, rupturing the burnt crust, writhing forth in scarlet molten ribbons.

Uplifted slabs of encrustation lie heaped in slices like charred meat. Dark red hornets, buzzard-large, drone through the haze, hunting their fellow doomed Carnations. These winged beasts were those who soothed their own inflamed and wretched souls by stinging others'.

In the Eternal Carnation, as in life, when they caught a hapless aspiring artist, they paralysed them by tarnishing their dreams, then implanted in their heart the larvae of despair. Hopeless, infested, the victim became food for the triumphing worm (or larva, if one wants to quibble).

The Caldera is home to both the poisonous and the poisoned. Those who brooded over past injustices until they festered, who stewed in self-pity, and scorched themselves with spite. It is a pestilential land, all ulcers and abscesses, carbuncles and canker.

One might say, the Empty Vessel is more enjoyable for that sort of thing.

For Pifflers merely grouse and drink, but the Picksores make of themselves a tavern for acrimony to dwell. They have not, like the Pasquinades, altered their creation for love or coin, but stained the very fibre of their Vision itself. Toxified it from within. And now it rots.

Artists who stooped to underhanded warfare, or those so enseethed at the successes of others' work, they neglected or corrupted their own. Those destroyed through notoriety which blossomed into narcissism, self-deification, and cruelty. Whose lack of recognition bred fury and resentment, or whose power led to tyranny and inhuman detachment, or whose grievances spawned a fixation upon revenge. All such emotions that cloud the Heart's Vision congeal in the Caldera of Scabs.

Button your coat.

THE BITTERNESS

G usting throughout the cavern is an acrid, metallic, dusty wind, redolent of hatred, envy, and self-loathing. It inflames the joints and sets a rage in the heart. In life, an artist catches wafts of the Bitterness now and then. A perceived inferior triumphs, a feckless layabout is drowned in millions. A subtly beautiful work is overlooked in favour of something more voguish or spangled.

Then the Bitterness creeps in.

Around the door locks it comes, during a splendid evening with companions, or in the dead of night whilst the artist lies awake, contemplating their own obscurity. They suddenly see favours where there are none, and intrigue rules the hour. Their perception narrows. They feel the whole world casts a cold eye upon their labours, determined to douse their flame. They cart the Bitterness around with them, spreading pestilence anew with every word as it sinks deep into their lungs and taints every breath. Eventually, they cannot distinguish it from their own scent. Their blood becomes bile, their tongue acidifies every taste. They drag traces of their universal disgust throughout the streets, aniseed to attract the hounds of a private hell.

THE SCABS

T read with care. If you poke through the upper layer with your foot, or sword, or walking stick, an evil-smelling liquid oozes from the puncture. If you bend and pluck at a corner of the burnt sienna crust, a slight warble emerges. Dig your fingers in and peel up an entire scab, and the plate pulls away with a mucosal sound. A rank cloud manifests with the breaking of the seal. A tremulous moan begins:

'O, what an unfortunate devil am I, O!'

'Do not pester the scabs!' Montcorbier may yell. But pester all you like. What does it matter now?

THE WRATHFOOL

rawling with ill-defined purpose, a cage of hands drags itself over the crust in a frenzied commotion of flesh and metal. Some hands stab each other with quills, or wound themselves with their own torn and blackened nails, some feverishly pluck feathers off fellow Carnations, whose carcasses they yet clutch. Other hands gesticulate, or claw the burning red surface through the bars.

The Wrathfool had been a master of bitter letters of complaint, poor reviews, and scathing comments. Indeed, this was all it ever wrote, which for a writer was not very productive.

Its disappointment with its life enraged it to such a degree that all it was capable of was destruction and the tearing down of others' happiness.

Impotent and raging, the Wrathfool leaves no furrow in the scabs, and all its fury ends in nothing.

Mercifully, now that it's Eternally Carnated, the sheer number of its complaints, each pulling this way and that, makes it somewhat limited in its perambulations.

THE SOULLESS FEAST

inking into the crust, a solid gold table is listing on the caldera. At one end perches an enormous, bloated, shiny red leech in a tight black suit.

It glistens with expensive oils. With monstrous delicacy, it dices smaller leeches on a golden platter, and sucks the pieces up into its churning orifice.

A Carnation consisting entirely of artificial smiles beams nastily at the display. Row upon row of gleaming, unconvincing teeth click up and down its body, overlapped like snake scales. It glows dimly in the malodorous smoke like a nightmare.

Nearby, a spindly platinum thing, draped in precious jewels, drinks molten metals. They overflow its mechanical mouth and pool amidst the scabs. In between gulps, it crunches sapphires, rubies, alexandrite, its gears jammed with gems.

At the end of the table, an artist is slowly being replaced by gold, cell by cell. Mostly gold already, it cannot speak. The gold creeps up from the table like frost. For despite the nauseating heat, the soulless feast is cheerless and cold.

THE INFAMOUS & ENFANT TERRIBLAH

o you hear a hooting in the distance? Behold, as a gibbering, slavering, blonde and red-faced baboon-like presence hurtles its way across the scabs, dragging its knuckles over the crust and its Vision battered and bruised behind it.

Its bulging body is clad in an ortolan-eggshell suit, and over one of its massive arms, looped with calculated casualness, a Birkin erupts with a tiny, frothing Pomeranian.

The Infamous screeches and pounds its fists on the table, scratches its fleas, and urinates copiously. Entrance made, it flings faeces at the other guests, and having dominated its audience, eats a Martini glass.

Meanwhile, abandoned under the table, a gigantic baby (although at death it was a millionaire in its fifties) swaddled in mink lies bawling.

Gifted with potential and a rare and delicate Vision, the Enfant Terriblah rose swiftly to fame, was pampered and flattered to within an inch of its fledgling life, then threw all its toys from the pram, along with its Vision, now sickly and thoroughly gummed over.

THE SELF-INFLATED

A tremendous blast of the Bitterness exhales over the land, and a great, tumescent blimp floats out above the scene. A Self-Inflated artist, its skin stretched taut over a frame at the end of its own tether, it is desperate to be looked at but is so unpleasant to see, that all avert their eyes. It hovers, lonely and malign, a blot on the corrupted sky.

THE GIMCRACK

estooned with medals and honours, the Gimcrack sparkles in the violent light. It grunts, and prises its bloodless torso apart like the segments of a withered orange.

Obsessed with garnering fame, its breast resembles the aftermath of a round of pin the tail on the donkey's arse. For each award, ribbon or decorative fancy it pulls away to hold up and admire, it also removes a section of chest. Eventually the whole falls away, its legs collapse, and the head bounces across the crust.

But never mind.

It happens all the time.

THE SWAMP

round the edges of the caldera the mephitic haze condenses, and the scabs putrefy into slime, forming a swamp from which colossal tropical growths emerge. Unripe fruit, like great ideas squandered through haste and a race for fame, lie sourly cast aside, untimely plucked and thus spoiled for eternal consumption. Strangler vines, like those which roam the above-ground city, wrap healthy trees in their ravenous embrace. The trees then suffocate and canker from within, rotting away to leave only the shape of their conqueror. Devoid of light, their buds wither, their potential for growth destroyed by envy's creeping clutch. Buds fallen, limbs wracked with worm and mould, the spiritless stems are now unfit even for kindling. These vines of resentment, jealousy, and self-pity twine up around any lost Carnations who might wander into the swamp, until they too rot from within. Among their decaying husks, a human scorpion with a tail full of black bile is a-scuttle, stabbing and spurting indiscriminately, whilst the Hermit Crabby, dragging its woes around with it, remains in its shell with its memories, stewing in misery.

By its side, the Octopoorus drowns in tears, tentacles flailing. Along the sodden ledge of the swamp, a Bombasneer crawls, spitting venom in the eye of anyone who dares look at it. The Languidstain, the colour of a boil, articulates its way over the roots, all its joints in motion. With a clatter it raises a swollen claw and drags a soggy cheroot to its intricate maw and inhales deeply, its carapace expanding. The wet cheroot smoulders, spits, sparks to life. On the exhale, the creature rotates a protruding eyeball around the swamp in a gaze of general vindictiveness.

Upon the banks, all manner of pestilence breeds. Mushroomed creatures spawn, and a parasitical fungus sprouts from the jaws of insectoid artists, seized with stillness, mid-action. An ant-like Carnation, its mandibles covered in lichen, with multiplicitous eyes the colour of peacock feathers, rises contorted from the swamp. From its head bursts a marvellous flower, scarlet and coralline. Its petals brush the ceiling of the sulphurous sky.

Alongside, an artist lies breathing steadily, its face lax, its chest a maze of fungus. Its every breath emits a sporal cloud, teeming and thriving. Another, an acid, pickled figure, wallows in the shallows. Its warty, bilious green skin is never soothed. It stinks of formaldehyde. Its grievances fester beneath the surface.

THE SECOND CODPIECE

owdered and bewigged, a languid toff lolls moodily in the swamp, over-plucked eyebrows arched in permanent dismay.

Its large stick-on beauty mark envelops half its face. The dank waters seep up and stain its white satin trousers. It holds a partially-eaten mouldy almond croissant, and sips from a bottomless sherry glass of yellowish bile.

The Second Codpiece was a forgotten thespian, and from it trickles a constant mutter about Capital City shows, nepotism, and 'that treacherous little whore of a director'.

THE PORCA MISERIA

owling at all it encounters is the Porca Miseria, born under an unlucky star, convinced its lot in life is to get the worst of everything. Shaped like an inverted horseshoe beneath its cloak, its face is a shattered mirror. One shard holds an eye, the other a nose, a third the corner of a sneer. As it moves, the expressions shift.

All are unpleasant.

A black cat weaves a demonic path around its iron legs as the Porca Miseria staggers through the swamp.

THE IMMORAL CRUSADER

ut look, O horror! The Immoral Crusader appears! White-robed and weeping, its gauzy frock is mottled with blood, trailing in the sodden scabs.

Underneath the shining guise of a pure and porcelain mask, it is loathsome to look at it, its soul contorted by private hatred. Beneath its saintly robes, the Immoral Crusader has a hidden axe to grind.

There are people it *dislikes*, for reasons of their birth, or romantic inclination, or self expression. It would see them dead. But it must cloak its desires in victimhood, so it swings a gilded sword around to combat invisible foes. Alas, the only ones it wounds are those unarmed and innocent.

I am in the right! it shouts. Yet all its actions are wrong. It has lost its comrades. Its job. Its dignity. Its rationality. Its milk of human kindness. But more pertinent to this guidebook, it has utterly destroyed its art, lost under the eternal outpouring of its vitriol.

History will avenge me! it cries, as it wanders, lonely, through its self-crafted hell.

THE MALADY-GO-ROUND

Unsettlingly cheerful music waltzes through the haze, and from out of the thick and gruesome fog a dreadful, lurid carousel appears, as bright as a smear of oil paint in the gloom. The haloes of gas lamps splutter in the greasy air, as the sound of the hurdy-gurdy, churning in the murk, winds up and down, pervading the swamp with a discordant, eerie, carnival ruckus.

Twisted brass poles puncture the canopy and pierce the blackened and grimy yellow sky like emaciated candy canes, as the carousel tilts and spins precariously.

Each artist is lashed to a differing steed like Ahab entangled with his whale.

One perches wrapped in prickly briars atop a gaunt and haggard nag, roped to it by lengths of putrid hide (poverty makes them ride thus!). Another lies plastered on the back of a sweaty, rotund, purebred white stallion, bound by strings of pearls (riches make them so ensnared!). Each artist rides the hobbyhorse of their predicament forever. The horrifying race goes round and round, and nobody will ever win, and all the whilst their Vision stamps its hooves waiting in the stalls.

THE THORNY DEVILS

B y the side of the carousel, Carnations dance around a giant thorn, glistening and ivory, shining with an unwholesome gleam, protruding from the mire like a morbid maypole. Each of them lug a similar, smaller thorn, piercing their side, the weight of it causing their steps to falter.

Would they not put down the thorn?

The devil they would.

For it is a pity party, held by those who coddled their canker. They found one weakness, one prick in the skin, one burr in their flesh, and fixated upon it all their lives. The tiny wound festered into a great pustule, and they grew around it, malformed. It became the justification for all ills and evils that befell their work.

'If only I didn't have this thorn in my side! I could do so many things!'

And they clutched that thorn to themselves feverishly. It was their only hope to escape dealing with their Vision. For how could they work when they were so burdened?

One artist wailed they were alone, and surely love would be a lifebuoy to their drowning muse?

Yet rather than seek companionship, or catharsis through art, or, gods forbid, revel in the strength of their isolation, they used their loneliness as a weapon to strike at people.

Another regarded the caring arm across their chest at night, a chain, dragging them down to a suffocating death. Their child's bright and scattered toys—a constellation that lights the way to mediocrity!

Aristocrats who thought their illustrious ancestry strangled them. No-names who felt hampered by their lack of one. An artist dwelling, by choice, in a remote corner of the world, or in the countryside, who howled about the tyranny of distance!

Some made their own beauty into their thorn:

'People have never seen my soul, for the obscuration of my wondrous face!'

And yet, this too plagued those whom life had gifted an unconventional visage.

Some made fame their crux to bear:

'My mansion upon the hill keeps all friendship in the valleys!'

You get the drift.

People fashioned thorns out of so many things.

And in the absence of external evils, they set in upon themselves. The only difference between these beings and the Underminers, is the latter isn't hiding from the truth.

These Thorny Devils were themselves the crafters of their torment, but cursed instead an imaginary, rotten thread in their line of fate, and beat not the weaver, but the loom.

Montcorbier knows well these residents. You'd hope so, mind. Else why is he the Guide to this unconscionable place?

That is the question.

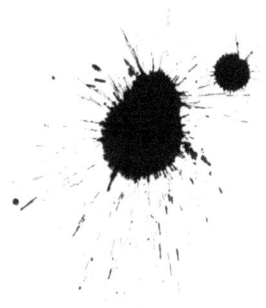

THE ARBITTER

residing over the Land of Scabs is the Arbitter, one of the oldest inhabitants of the City of Lost Intentions.

With paper twisted in its hair, misery twisted in its eye, and scorn coiled in its brain like a snake, the Arbitter dwells within a black pot of green bile. Sharp and skeletal, dripping with poison, in life it had failed at its own work, so spent its dwindling (then sharply truncated) years attacking the work of others. Its yellow carnation, wizened and blackened, hangs limp upon its cadaverous chest. An effluence of disappointment rolls off it. The Bitterness has seeped deep into the fibres of its heart and made them rank.

It mainly rants insensibly, but if you listen to this herpetic quagmire long enough, it will tell you of a creature worse than itself.

A creature who is the cause of all the suffering in the City of Lost Intentions. A puppet tangled in his own strings. A night-walker trapped in a city eternally at noon. The detested lord of his own kingdom, and the monster at the heart of a self-crafted labyrinth.

Woeful being, he once mocked death, thinking death mocked life. Why bother to guard one's treasures, said he, when death robbed all at end?

So he was careless with his work. Ignored his Heart's demands that he be vigilant, and listened only to Reason, which told him all was meaningless.

He grew dissolute, gambled away his fortune. After years of dissipation, his Heart buried beneath the chaff of wasted days, drowned in the dregs he drank, he finally achieved his end. We will not say how, for that is his affair. But suffice to say, all did not go according to plan.

For he hadn't reckoned on the degree to which the Heart governs the soul. That even unto death, the soul is still the Heart's prerogative. And his Heart damned him for his disrespect. When at last death came to trap him, his Heart tricked death, and threw its ungrateful owner into his own creation:

The land of the Eternal Carnation.

He washed up on the broken shores of the Inkspill Sea outside the City of Lost Intentions. He didn't know where he was at first, and assumed some flummoxy of the brain, disporting itself as it perished. But in truth, he was caught within an endless moment of self-reckoning.

He looked into his innermost core and saw only betrayal. He could not pardon himself for what he had done, or failed to do, with his life's work, but also for what he *had* created, and so he has remained in the Eternal Carnation ever since, suffering the everlasting vengeance of his Heart.

He, who had thought death rendered life devoid of meaning, was cursed with immortality. This cruel joke played by his Heart upon his soul has worn thin as the years stole by.

And what is his life now but a perpetual palimpsest? Each day scrapes itself blank and writes itself anew, but it is always the same page, and the story never alters.

He wanders through a scaffold-ridden dream of the empire he neglected to build.

The Vision he failed.

He tires of the fact that among the miscellany of beings in the Eternal Carnation, only he truly suffers. He would end it all himself, if he could.

For he is at heart an Underminer. A saboteur.

And of all the creatures in this unpardonable place, the most unpardonable.

We are speaking, of course, about the Architect of this wretched city.

We shall get to the blackguard shortly.

Poisoning

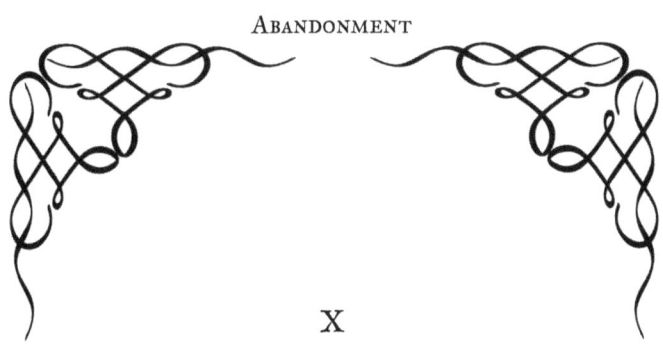

X

THE HOARSE LATITUDES

PERILOSTS

Abandonment of Art

ATOP A FOG-COVERED MOUNTAIN RANGE RISING FROM THE EDGE OF THE CALDERA, A BRONZE HORN BLOWS DESPAIRINGLY.

Tendrils of hopelessness curl in the maudlin notes. A lamenting cry, calling for all to join in a battle already lost. Climb towards the mournful sound, following the Guide.

As you ascend, more and more of the rotten trees will topple. Fetid tropical foliage will give way to bare and brittle stalks, trunks of fossilised trees, and stripped, snow-topped branches.

229

Up high, the air loses its humid stench and becomes thin and cold, stabbing at the lungs with each breath.

But another vapour is drifting up from the valley beyond the mountains, wrapping around the climber like a wet silk scarf.

This is the Haartache, a dank, dark fog of tears. With a scent of fear and failure, it makes the heart pound arrhythmically, and starts a hysterical flutter in the chest. Yearning is its top note, loss its middle, terror its base.

Don't breathe too deeply, or a petrifying melancholy will transfix you.

THE KNIGHT AT THE CROSSROADS

pon the crest, a lapidified figure waits. A stone knight on a stone horse, looking into nothingness. A lace of frost and lichen obscures its features. Its granite torso is blackened, and ice has spread along the seams of its carved armour, prising it open like a clam shell. Crystalline fingers creep down the legs of its haggard steed.

Before the pair, a headstone emerges crookedly from the iced earth, the name illegible and worn. The knight's shield, also, is indecipherable with age. Having lost its muse, the knight no longer believed anything was worth fighting for, so its quest disappeared, along with the sun.

THE LAST PIPER

Further along the ridgeline, a lone Piper stands between the splintering trees, yearning for battles to glorify with song. Its pipes, protruding from the collapsed bag of its chest, hang limp.

Wistful for the past, deflated and bowed, every breath it draws, a trembling groan. There is mildew on its tartan.

THE STAGNANT SEA

n the valley, masts disappear and reappear in the mist like spectres. They rise from a shallow, cloud-hung, inland sea, cluttered with collapsed galleons, broken barquentines, and angular, twisted caravels, the ships of those who have lost their bearings.

From afar, their array makes a ghostly forest, half-hidden amid the dense whiteness.

The Guide will lead the way down the mountain towards the shore. You may clutch the back of his tattering coat as you slide over the ice-slick boulders and crunch through stalagmites of frigid gorse, encircled all the while by the grieving Haartache.

THE SORROWBOUND

ear the shoreline the waters harden. Shards of glassy blue file up against each other in sheaves of delicate, deadly beauty, like the sweepings of a broken window.

A tinkling as of a wind chime, and a more ominous cracking echoes around the crescent shore, muffled by the fog, as the surface relentlessly heaves and fights.

Abandoned sculptures, hewn from slabs of glacier, lie amidst the scattered ice, their agonised sculptors preserved within them. Haggard, sorrowful faces, glazed behind hundreds of layers of mica-thin aquamarine. Fragile, hedged in, shattered. Here are those whose grievous memories had crept through their work, and turned them to ice.

A statue made of deep blue whorls of ancient water stares sightlessly inward. Alienly beautiful, its haunted face ageless and androgynous. The sculpture's tears have hardened on its crystal-dusted cheekbones. Though incomplete, it is already alive. Its arms embrace its sculptor, frozen to its breast.

THE HOARSE LATITUDES

he forest of masts, first seen from the ridge, stands silent in the fog bank. A graveyard of ships, stretched out into eternity, a-tilt and wrecked in the lifeless waters.

Ruptured, corrupted steamers, devoured by rust, stained ochre by the iron oxide sludge which pours from the buckled portholes like blood, lie among warped wooden hulls perched skeletally on the reef, draped in rotted sails, the bone-coloured canvas turning black with damp.

The sea has become a sterile lagoon. Bloated, yellow, poisonous fish float dead in the brine. You must wade through the corrosive murk, strips of feathery seaweed entangling your legs, the leathery plant licking up and winding slimily around your waist. Blistery, sour-looking sea grapes swim amidst the dark strands.

Montcorbier won't carry you. Don't ask him.

A tall ship is beached on a shoal in the stale fog of the Haartache. Creep, if you will, through the breach in the barnacled, algae-overtaken hull. The ship is full of despondent adventurers, befugged by laudanum, all unresponsive and hopeless. Blanketed by lichen and rot, the lost explorers no longer look for land.

They were the artists who simply succumbed to despair and did nothing, allowing their Vision to stagnate. Stuck without wind, they failed to realise they must row themselves out.

And now they have lost their oars, eaten by shipworm.

THE BILGE

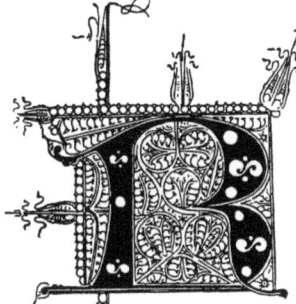

otting in its namesake, the Bilge sits below the waterline.

So consumed by its belief in life's lack of romanticism and adventure that it doesn't even bother to unfurl what remains of the sails. The lack of monsters has rendered the sea unworthy.

The Bilge is sunk in filth up to its neck. The oily surface quivers around its jaw. It submerges a little deeper, and rancid water laps into its quavering mouth. Its eyes are dull. It can no longer speak. Parasites run rampant over its scalp. Lank hanks of long hair trail in the gizzards of the sea.

Whose ship is this?

It is the captain's ship, obviously.

And who has left the captain here?

The captain has left themselves. They have no star to sail by. A captain with no star is equally unfortunate as one with no wind. Nothing will save them now. They've let the waters in for far too long …

THE KEELHAUL

ashed to the hull of the ship is the Keelhaul. Strands of seaweed cling clammily to the figurehead's pallid skin, the swollen fibres of the ropes sinking tenderly into its codfish flesh. It is stippled with barnacles whose edges fissure into wounds.

The Keelhaul had wished to suffer for its art, until eventually, believing there was no point to anything, it merely suffered. Waterlogged and sensitive, it hangs from its tarred harness, eyes bulbous and jellied.

THE SIGHREN

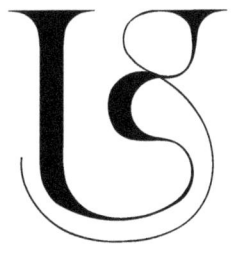pon a jagged rock perches the Sighren, wan and weary, with no desire to sing. The stone has crept up from beneath and petrified all it touches. The claws of the Sighren are stone already. Its feathers, heavy as marble.

Montcorbier sometimes lies down next to it.

Neither speak.

There is no further.

The land curves up again in half a mile. You crawl through a hole in the underground firmament and come out on the far side of the mountain city. Beyond the ink moat lies the salt lake, and beyond that, endless desert.

And beyond the desert?

Somebody else's story. Freedom.

Or nothing. I'm not sure.

It's not really my area.

Words, words ...

Let us dry the despair of our bones in the sands.

And now, at last, the end.

For one of us.

THE SALT LAKE

DEEP IN THE VAST AND SHIMMERING WHITE SALT LAKE THAT LIES BEYOND THE CITY, A BLACKENED THORN TREE RISES, A CLAW AGAINST THE SKY.

The dead tree offers no shelter. And yet, beneath it, a figure sits.

He sits and writes in a book. A book of curling ink-stained pages. Poorly bound.

No longer the splendid lotus-eater who greets the new arrival—Montcorbier looks ill.

The sun has raised blisters on his sallow face, leaving roses and crimson crescents of peeling skin upon his cheekbones. His eyes are raw rimmed and desolate, and his coat has tattered out into ribbons, like the tail of a gaunt and threadbare lyrebird, feathers trailing in the dust.

By the end, he always looks like this.

But soon Montcorbier must begin again. Make another gruelling tour through the city.

It is a cursed cycle.

Occasionally he stops writing, puts his head upon his knees, and shuts his eyes. Or with trembling hands plucks a twig from the littered ground, where, around his folded form, scattered branches lie.

Half a forest of bark has, by his feverish fingers, been stripped away.

The sun is, as ever, at its height.

It is eerily still on the boundary of the Eternal Carnation. The walls of the glass dome that enclose the city stretch up over the salt lake. Sand particles from the deeper desert beyond the dome glance off its outer surface to create a scene like an inverted snow-globe. At the base of this invisible barrier, piles of dull grey powder form small dunes.

On the far side of the city, towards the Inkspill Sea, the fog bank hovering on the shoreline curls over the curved shoulder of the glass like a shawl.

A tableau of salt statues, phantoms in the heat, kneel upon the baked ground as though struck down by the sun whilst advancing across the lake. Some have their hands up, wielding off an unseen foe. Others have been arrested in the act of rising to their feet. They bear crowns of jagged, translucent spikes, and salt-lace hangs off their stiffened limbs and creeps upwards in a foliage of crystals.

Looking back at the city, you can watch Carnations crawl over its crumbling towers and wander the overgrown streets like garish insects. Faint in the baking air, a cry drifts down from the Colonauseam, followed by a thrumming of drums. The silver and gold onion domes glint in the desert light, their scales tarnished. Between the salt lake and the mountain, the black moat glistens, and Peregrinators in their ink-pot skiffs are pulled round and round forever.

And it is here we end our journey. Or rather, you do.

I shall remain.

Here, in the City of Lost Intentions, under an eternal magnifying glass. For that is what it truly is.

And what, truly, am I?

The Guide?

Yes. For my sins, quite literally.

For I am also, alas ...

THE ARCHITECT

I have been here for over two centuries, or thereabouts. It's difficult to measure. Over two hundred years since the day of the fire, when I washed up on the shores of the Inkspill Sea.

I assure you, I recognised where I was in a ghastly instant. Don't believe that malignant Arbitter in the swamp. No, in a flash, I knew the hell was mine. The hell I had written in Montmartre, in a garret wood-walled like a coffin.

The poignant and ridiculous Carnations, or Predicaments, with their alliterative Ps. The Temple of Fo-Elpmet-Eht. The Undermine ... The wretched Misery Makars. All of them my creations.

And I realised I was guilty of all crimes against my Heart. If you look in the Bookmark's record of Misdeeds, you will find my own.

Name: Montcorbier de Mock-Sombre (or so I called myself in my idiot youth).

Peccati:

Avoidance

Neglect

Infidelity

Diminishment

CONTORTION

DESECRATION

BETRAYAL

SABOTAGE

POISONING

ABANDONMENT

I can, of course, elaborate.

Avoidance, because it should truly not have taken ten years to write a work so flimsy.

Neglect, because I piffled away my talents through endless prattling in the bars and salons.

Infidelity, because I am a hedonist. A wine-drenched soak of a man, or whatever I am.

Diminishment, because I changed my book from ye olden language to normalese. Easier to read, but it went against my Heart.

Contortion, because who is so ridiculously pedantic as to bother to classify artistic peccadillos in the first place?

Desecration, because only a ghoul or an especially morbid type would spend their years crafting a hell rather than somewhere more pleasant.

Betrayal, because I allowed my philosophical system to bully me into building a throne for it and then to contrive a servile narrative at the expense of good literature.

Sabotage, yes, very much so. Horrifically so.

First through undermining myself with drink, and then through an act of thoughtlessness which resulted in the quite spectacular destruction of my work when my papers went up in flames. Whoosh! The lot. Including my allegory ... Most particularly my allegory.

Poisoning, because, for all my feigned detachment, fancying myself perched insouciantly upon a mountain, surveying humanity like a god, I am in truth something of a bastard, and my irritation with the world filtered through my pen and stained the pages.

Abandonment ... no, I suppose, I did not abandon my art. It may, however, have been better if I had. And regardless, circumstances—largely self-orchestrated—ensured it abandoned *me*.

Thus, as my book was in tatters when it was set ablaze, so the city is. An unfinished, poorly sketched cartoon. I wrote it to terrify myself into industry. Internal judgement in the absence of eternal laws. I conjured a sea and filled it with monsters.

Because, how better to spur yourself on to write or paint than create a hell that awaits you if you dally and prevaricate?

And yet I dallied and prevaricated.

And then I died. Rather, first I lost my manuscript to fire. You'd think a drunken accident, a lamp left burning. But no. Only half so. It was, at end, the unhappy placement of a magnifying glass.

Like a child, that fateful night I'd been watching weevils. Sprawled upon the floor with my magnifying glass and bottle. (For yes, of course I was drinking.)

When eventually I, feckless sot, crawled to bed, I tossed the glass upon my cloak, discarded on a chair—the chair by the window, it is pertinent to add, near a low table strewn with my dusty, wine-stained papers—and then I thought no more, entering the dreamless slumber of the self-stupefied.

In the morn, after I'd staggered into the streets, the sun shone through the glass's lens, focused its cruel and piercing eye upon a curling corner of my hellish work, and judged it wanting. Set fire to it, ignited page after page, like a row of beacons signalling my failure.

I can only surmise this is what happened. I returned to a roomful of smoke, an accusatory mound of ash upon the copper tabletop, and the culprit, gleaming amid the velvet folds of my preposterous evening wear.

That which I feared, my poor Locksmith's fate, the losing of my life's work, and thus my life, I brought into being. It came to my summoning.

In the days that followed, I could only drag myself around. A shambles of a man. A husk. I couldn't think on it. When I tried, my mind recoiled, like a thing accustomed to darkness thrust violently into the light.

In this state I made some ... acquaintances, at the card table.

I think I died fairly soon after being thrown in the pit. I broke something. A few things, probably. Being, as ever, rather drunk, I felt little. A small mercy.

As I was dying, I watched the pit's telescoped circle of stars fade and fill with morning sky. By noon, this lens centred with that pitiless sun.

Then the pain began. I knew it was the end.

But then! Whilst I lay wallowing in black water, in underground stench, ornamented with rats, a version of myself appeared. Another I in like array—my Heart— and this tattered pomp, this knowing reprobate—my mirror me—in filthy beauty garbed, put his ungloved fingers round my throat, and, squeezing, clasping hard, did ask:

'Anything to say to your Heart, wretch, to save yourself from its damnation?'

And I, perverse fool, answered:

'See you in hell.'

(In retrospect, an unwise thing to say.)

And here I am. Borne so swift and silent to this gaudy grave of my own creation. Imprisoned in the art I willed to walk upon the earth in my absence.

Cursed with immortality for wasting my life.

In the insensible company of those given unspeakable, unfathomable existence by me. The Jackofall, the Millineed, the Golden Lion, the Martingale, that miserable beast the Arbiter. Even the Palimpsest.

They are creatures born of my fears and foibles. And I, trapped on stage with them, in an endless, infernal play. For I cannot leave the boundaries of the city. The glass imprisons me as it does my creations. Whatever gets too close turns to ash. Even I. But I return. I always do. Like some godforsaken phoenix.

The years passed, and I resigned myself to my fate.

I had little alternative, mind.

But then, a horrible, yet wondrous event! It seemed my private hell filled a public need for self-damnation. For soon, real artists arrived. Not from my pen. Some emerged as new Carnations, strange and increasingly mysterious to me, as outside the zeitgeist changed. But others mere penitential tourists, one might say.

Not dead. Not yet. But those who had felt the first shadow of their Heart's disfavour, whose souls were sent here as a warning. They washed up on the shores of the Inkspill Sea, with all the detritus of their forgotten art.

After my initial delight, my misanthropic self's surprising, aching relief at the presence of fellow humans, I didn't know what to do with them.

How could I reveal they'd plummeted into the trap I'd laid only for myself? And that there was no return journey because my book wasn't finished when I *inconveniently* died? Absurd! So, I led the first artist through the city to the salt lake.

What else was I to do?

She panicked when my courage made its belated entrance and I confessed the nature of the place. Fluttered like a butterfly in a bell jar, beating against the walls. And then, oh horror, when she touched the glass, she turned to ash.

I can see it still. The next one was arguably worse. He took flight and turned to salt. Frozen whilst fleeing across the lake. Another sinless insect held captive in the eye of my self-examining glass.

To the third, I told the truth outside the city gates, imprudently near the moat. They immediately fell upon me. Tried to drown me in the ink.

They drowned instead.

I kept my silence after that. I learned if I abandoned these visitors inside the city, they turned into Carnations. Not fully formed ones, like those who arrived here after death, but uncertain, hybrid things, born of their many potential futures, who wandered nebulously around the streets.

Of course, the Underseer found them. I thought it kinder, therefore, to lead them to the salt lake, and then depart. I play-acted the role of Guide for so long that eventually I fell asleep in my mask, so to speak.

But I remember them.

The sculptor who'd chosen to sculpt their marriage instead. The songwriter lost in a barren, money-strewn landscape. The academic who'd allowed bitterness to swallow them whole. The cantankerous novelist who'd drunk themselves into the remainders bin. The actor who'd forgotten to leave a ghost light on for their soul.

They all turned to salt or fell as ash. I failed to lead any of them out again. I am, ironically, not a very good guide to my creation.

The original Poet of my manuscript died here as well. I wrote them up until the salt lake, then the garret fire took them away before I could write them a boat to leave in, to sail back to life. But they were a lovely being. Their death too lies at my darkened door. They weren't here when I arrived. I don't know where the original Guide is either, the villain. While the hell remains, the chief actors are missing. I expect that's why we play their parts.

God knows who I am writing to.

I make amendments to this guidebook, here on the salt lake. Hunched like a vulture, or sprawled like a spineless tome under the shadeless acacia, scratching with my quill upon the yet unburned pages, pilfered from the Bookmark.

When I am done, I shall give it back to the devil, and it can fill it with its beloved typefaces and fiddly bits. Then *something* will be finished in this impossible city.

Shortly I must return to the Inkspill Sea and collect another artist. Drag them up and down the mountain, then watch them turn to salt or ash, like all the rest.

So, I'm afraid to say, unlikely reader, that if you ever find yourself here with me, are upon this final stage with me, that there is no exit through the wings.

But would you have followed me had I told the truth of what awaited you at curtainfall? Would you not have ended your story there, preferring to drown in the Inkspill Sea? What would be the point of that?

We all return to the sea in the end, metaphorically, but in the meantime, why not head inland? Spend your one gold coin? Pen your solitary, death-bound play?

At least we've had a lark.

It's better than nothingness.

And if the land you long for does not exist—create it, like a mapmaker raising imaginary mountains from the shoals. A new coastline is added to the charts, around which ships then plot and steer their way. Thus does the Heart outwit Reason. And though 'tis mere fantasy, the world is richer for it.

Perhaps, though, also, I was lonely.

What else was I meant to do with my endless day?

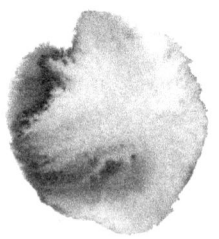

POSTAMBLE

ow you have come this far, and I have ruined the mood, it may all seem gloomy. But don't despair!

Perhaps one day a hapless artist, fallen to their self-crafted doom, *will* escape? Perhaps their Heart will forgive them so utterly that it plucks them from this oubliette and hurls them back to life, as in that dismal pit, mine might have saved me from myself.

Perhaps they will take this fiasco of a manuscript with them, and let it be a guide to those at risk of losing their intentions.

Conceivably, one day, my Heart may also forgive *me*. And on that day ... if such a day occurs ... I can see it so clearly. Because I may have been drunk for the idea, but I will be sober for *this* execution!

From the distance there comes a whispering of sand. What seems, for a cruel moment, to be a sail on the horizon. Scudding across the dunes, and onto the salt lake. White upon white. Slicing the air. A scythe, raised.

The Palimpsest moves like a flash, and the crescent of light cuts me down with the ringing peal of a glass harp. In a flurry of coattails and billowing parchment, both I and the Palimpsest disappear. My wretched yellow carnation falls to the ground.

Then!

A tremendous gong strikes! The land shakes, and the city trembles. Rumbling tremors wrack the foundations, and squawks and screeches pierce the air as winged Carnations take frantic flight, and the moat of ink boils over.

The city groans and seems to bulge, inflating, whilst a roaring and babbling of voices rises higher and higher in the heat. Finally, with the sound of monstrous fibres tearing apart, the city bursts open like a spider's egg!

Out pours a roiling mass of Carnations, thousand upon thousand, my fellow prisoners, clambering over the ruins, darting out from the crumbling stone, down to the smoking shores of the Inkspill Sea.

The walls of the city ignite!

The flags curl up like flaming flowers against the bruised and luminous backdrop of the plummeting sun.

The dome over the eternal city shatters! The sky cracks open, and into the freed land whirls an exhilarating wind, dispersing the fog bank before it like a sinister puff of smoke blown from a shadowed alley.

The blackened vines which have strangled the city swell with sap and spring to life. Green shoots erupt into leaves and tendrils, and great tropical blooms glow against the rapidly darkening sky.

Over the smouldering ruins of the Colonauseam, the fires sink back like genies into their bottles. Charred mildew drops off the pagodas, the Vainguardians throw down their swords, the gargoyles right themselves, and the rot and patina draws back like a tide, leaving a shining broken city against the burgeoning stars.

An unknown stillness comes over the land.

A jungle grows among the ruins, and spreads out into the desert, a sprawling, lush oasis. The Giraffagon wanders the undergrowth, eating the lurid blossoms, and the Golden Lion strolls the winding, wonky streets.

From the ruptured H'Auditorium, the empty evening suits and gowns spill out into the night air and blow away, the Limelight flies up to meet the moon, and I am not there at all, but from high on the mountain comes drifting down to the Inkspill Sea and across the black water the sound of the Heart's forgiveness.

Hearken! It is a joyful fandango of violins and castanets!

A. Valliard is an allegorist, ex-bookseller, ink scribbler, painter, occasional ham actor, and permanent resident of the City of Lost Intentions.

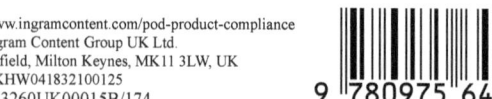